Praise for Charles Chadwick's *It's All Right Now*:

'This novel is huge – in size (obviously), ambition, intelligence and heart'

Jonathan Safran Foer

Satisfying and beautiful... Chadwick is excellent at catching speech patterns and personal traits; many of his characters are repulsively or absurdly fascinating, and Ripple's vexed relationship with his children is masterfully evoked'

The Herald

'Exhilarating... brilliant... radically original'

David Gates, *Newsweek*

'At once modern and epic... funny, moving... and rather casually magnificent'

Ben Kunkel, *Los Angeles Times Book Review*

'Remarkable... a vivid picture of how one unfashionable man can end up touching the lives around him, including the reader's own'

People Magazine

'Ripple's inner world blossoms on the page with writing that drives the reader onward'

Wyatt Mason, *Harper's Magazine*

'Chadwick's achievement is such that Ripple's small thoughts – slight observations, petty miseries, daily regrets – come to seem worthy of centre stage'

The New Yorker

'A gripping narrative...Ripple is an observant and self-deprecating interpreter of both the lavish gallery of characters and the ever-hanging times'

Guardian

A Chance Acquaintance

A Chance Acquaintance

CHARLES CHADWICK

Published in 2009 by
Short Books
3A Exmouth House
Pine Street
London EC1R 0JH

10 9 8 7 6 5 4 3 2 1
Copyright ©
Charles Chadwick 2009

A CIP catalogue record for this book
is available from the British Library.

ISBN 978-1-906021-40-5

Printed in the UK by Clays, Suffolk

Jacket design and photography: Richard Jenkins

For Caroline

I

DOROTHY SAT at her father's desk. Henry had let her have it – at a price – adding it to her share of their father's estate. It was just like Henry. Worth at least two thousand pounds, he said. Oh no it wasn't. And now he'd sent her a pompous letter about selling the cottage. She glanced at the mirror over the mantelpiece and smiled, practising it for Elsie, who would be there soon. It was never right – kind, welcoming even, but how much love was there in it? The mirror was too high for Elsie to see herself in it. Her smile turned into a mask of bitterness. The hair she had had done that morning was a ridiculous wonky silver helmet. One of the women at the bridge morning – Gladys, was it? – once told her she had an austere look. She wished she had a different, more long-lasting smile for Elsie after all these years.

She would give her another cheque, to help with

her little expeditions to visit gardens. She wanted to be sure that wasn't why she came. Perhaps it was out of duty. How could she guess what love there might be in it, for it could not show on her face. And on her own, what was there to see? Anxiety. Shame. She'd always tried to stand by Elsie when she was a child. How often had she told her that looks are nothing, all that matters is what people are like underneath? Elsie had stopped crying when she was about eight, having got used to herself.

She wasn't as worried as she used to be. Elsie had her cleaning work and her visits to gardens and her comfy little flat. She'd chosen the material and made the curtains for it, as mothers should. There was the television, of course. She'd paid for her to have driving lessons and she was ready to pass the test. She'd passed the written part of it, but kept on putting off the practical side. Perhaps she was nervous about people getting a glimpse of her and the danger of causing an accident. It wouldn't be the same without an instructor sitting beside her. That was all there was to her life. Without love or excitement in it. There was nothing to be worried about. Nothing would happen to Elsie now, just having to be herself, day after day.

She couldn't forget the question Gladys asked while she dealt the cards after failing to get in touch with the blessed Arthur for Mavis. Arthur was the most boring man she had ever known. Gladys reached him three times and each time he only wanted to tell

Mavis not to forget to water the geraniums. That was how boring Arthur was. Mavis had to remind them for the umpteenth time that he was the forgetful one and she'd never forgotten to water a flower in her whole life, not once.

She went into the kitchen to prepare a tea tray. She wanted Elsie to feel this would always be her home. The question Gladys asked was whether she would have had Elsie killed in her womb if she'd known how she would turn out. That wasn't fair. It was hard to be fair to Gladys, or any of the other women for that matter. What Gladys actually said, very casually as she dealt the last few cards, was: 'One can't help wondering if it would have been better if certain people had never been born.' Admittedly, they'd been talking about the gangs of youths who'd been terrorising a nearby housing estate. She'd looked at Gladys very closely to see if she would give her one of her glances, a hint that the question might include Elsie. But she didn't. The others began looking at the cards they'd been dealt. Applying the same question to Elsie would have been in their minds too. It was Mavis who glanced at her but she was her partner and that was probably to get a clue of what sort of a hand she had. Mavis had nodded at what Gladys had said. Mavis and Arthur had had no children, from giving all their attention to those geraniums, no doubt.

Elsie would be there in half an hour. She was always on time. You had to be punctual at the hospital, she'd explained, to find out what your duties were each day and collect your mop and broom and materials. Dorothy brought out the china she'd inherited from her father. Henry had put a price on that too – best Spode. The point was that Gladys had not put the thought into her head, had only reminded her that it was there already, skulking in the undergrowth. Perhaps everyone's mind was like that: a part that is lit up in the daily business of thinking and living, and a dark, shadowy hinterland where all sorts of nastiness were waiting to pounce. She had read somewhere about a 'common pool of humanity which everyone shares'. She knew that feeling from her charity work. But there was a cesspool of humanity that was common to everyone too.

When Elsie came, it was difficult to give a frank and loving smile with the shame of that question slithering around in her mind. So she tried to keep busy, pottering about and making tea or hoping for an excuse to turn the television on. She thought of Elsie boarding a bus and the looks she would get. It was awful to lump her together with those horrible thugs. She had never done any harm to anyone. If anyone didn't share that cesspool it was Elsie. She was used to people staring or looking away. Some people, if they were born like that, would boil over with rage and resentment. Perhaps Elsie did too sometimes. Perhaps she was overcome with hatred. She did not know. She had never known. As Elsie grew up, she would sometimes suddenly say she was going up to her room to lie down. That was after the tears stopped and there was no other way of knowing that something, usually at school, had made her specially unhappy. The teachers had done their best, but as one of them tried to explain, it was difficult to penetrate her loneliness. She'd left as soon as she was allowed to, with only three GCSEs, and stayed at home, getting menial jobs here and there, until she got a flat of her own.

She would change into more comfortable clothes for Elsie, to introduce a note of informality. She wondered if Elsie ever thought she was lucky to be alive, that her mother hadn't had her done away with before she was born. It had been a horrible birth, as if Elsie already knew that life might not be worth living. Sometimes Dorothy thought she detected a look of gratitude in that grim, warped face. There were no expressions she could make that did not give her a more sinister look. Elsie grateful to her. Grateful! At least she wasn't her only child. At least she had Geoffrey. She went into the bedroom to choose more relaxed-looking clothes, then thought better of it. 'I'm sorry, Elsie,' she said. 'I really am.' But for what, for not knowing how to give her a loving, motherly smile? She must make her feel at home. She mustn't go on about her leg which, anyway, was better now.

II

ELSIE FACED the window of the bus so as not to put people off sitting next to her. It wasn't as if nobody ever wanted to talk to her, just off the cuff, once they'd got used to her. Occasionally, anyway. They didn't think she was likely to pass it on to anybody else. They couldn't imagine her having a good old gossip with somebody at a bus stop or on a street corner. It was as if she was hardly a person at all. She always wanted to know more about people and tried not to stare. She wanted people to get to know her better. Her mother had told her umpteen times that what mattered lay underneath. That was what she had often told herself.

She had learnt as a child to stop the hatred welling up and taking her over. But sometimes it still seized her as if it was always there waiting to pounce. Sometimes it was when she saw some pretty young people flaunting themselves. Or the faces in the advertisements for make-up and clothing and hair-dos. People too pleased with themselves. It didn't last. The devil had done his dirty work and had enough satisfaction in life without bothering with her.

They had to sit next to her when the bus was crowded, leaning forward with their shopping or other things clutched on their laps, after glancing at her once. If they looked twice, it might be because they were desperate to talk to anybody. On a long journey it was harder not to, with arms touching.

A man sat next to her. He smelt of something sour and sweet at the same time, of something being covered up. She couldn't stop glancing at him, guessing.

'What are you staring at?' he said angrily.

His throat needed clearing. Perhaps he kept it like that to give it a husky sound. His head had been shaved and the hair was growing back patchily, black with grey in it. His shoes were highly polished and his trousers were sharply creased. She noticed things like that when people might have something to prove. It was the greyness of him, the lines crisscrossing around his eyes, though he didn't seem old otherwise. She looked at him a moment longer, her curiosity getting the better of her.

Then he said, 'I killed a bloke, if you must know. Did fifteen years. Out four months. And now you can stop fucking staring at me.'

Elsie was grateful to him. He wouldn't have told

anyone else that, not out of the blue. His eyes were grey too and glared at her, as if waiting for her to look shocked or frightened. She didn't make expressions if she could help it. Smiles, for example. Hers looked like snarls, the worse the more friendly they were. It was the way her teeth jutted out, the bottom ones. And her eyes so deep in her head you could hardly see them. She had practised in the mirror for hours but it only made her look as if she hated herself. A preacher on television had once said that people should look in the mirror and tell themselves that God loved them. She'd tried that several times and decided that if God existed, that must be true, but loving would be easy for him without any alternative. She didn't hate herself except when the devil made her hate other people too. She could find things comical when she wanted to. Though when she laughed she looked as if she was gasping for air. She was excellent at not showing her feelings because that was when her face let her down most. So she kept it blank. That was why people trusted her, just came out with it and told her they'd killed someone. So she said, 'Oh yes?' As if he'd told her he'd caught a cold the previous winter or something very run-of-the-mill like that.

But he'd lost interest and looked out of the other window. She was sorry she might have appeared rude, so after two stops she asked, 'Why did you do that?'

It seemed the polite thing to ask. But he only replied, 'Mind your own fucking business.'

People sometimes addressed her like that as if she would be too stupid to mind, as if there was nothing much else she could mind, looking like that. 'Unprepossessing' her mother had called it once. That wasn't quite fair. 'Not very prepossessing' were her actual words. She'd overheard her mother saying it on the telephone, that was all. It wasn't to her face. Her mother couldn't help looking at her as if she wished she was different, more like Geoffrey.

On the spur of the moment she said, 'I've sometimes felt like killing my mother. Or my father come to that.'

She was on her way to see her mother, so that was what came into her head. It wasn't true. It was a friendly thing to say, to keep the conversation going, putting herself in the same boat. She wished she had a jokey smile to go with it.

But he only muttered, 'Stupid ugly bitch!'

So much for being considerate. She did try when the opportunity arose. She did want to get on the right side of people instead of putting them off the whole time. There wasn't really an alternative.

They got off at the same stop. Once she turned round because she thought he was following her, it crossing her mind she might be his next victim, though she'd probably be the last person in the whole world anyone would want to murder. Anyway, he was nowhere to be seen.

She didn't hurry along the street, keeping to the

shadows cast by the summer trees. She didn't even know if her mother liked her and looked forward to her visits. She couldn't think of any reason why she should. Perhaps she thought it was only what children did... There were some pretty front gardens, mostly with roses past their best, needing to be pruned. They had a stifled look as though they were gathering dust in the summer sun.

She had once seen a photograph of her parents' wedding. Her mother wasn't exactly a portrait painting, not even when she made the best of herself. She sometimes sat stretched back in her armchair with her leg up on a poof, showing it off to be complained about. And sometimes she leant back her head, showing her neck. It was true: she'd once caught herself wondering if it would be easy to throttle her or if there were too many fatty wrinkles. As she turned into her mother's street and there were fewer shadows cast by the trees, she couldn't stop herself wondering if the man on the bus would do it for ten thousand pounds. The last time her mother had complained about her leg and never looked at her, or only once, as if straight-away regretting it. Her father had looked at them from the wedding picture as if disappointed with them both. She hadn't stayed long, not after her mother got on to the subject of her leg. 'What could you be in a hurry for?' she had asked. There were those thoughts that slipped into her head when she wasn't on the look-out for them. Most of the time she just wished she was different so that her mother wouldn't have to try so hard to love her.

She could talk about her new job. She'd had quite a few, of the cleaning variety. She wasn't a fool by any stretch of the imagination but people weren't to know that. Once she'd applied for a job at a big department store. There were two of them, a man and a woman, with an earnest kindness and smartly dressed in dark suits. On the form she'd said her preference was for the cosmetics department. She'd only done it for a laugh, to see the look on their faces. They were very polite and kept a straight face throughout. They asked about her previous experience in the retail trade. Which was precisely nil. Ditto her knowledge of make-up. She did not use it herself. It would be like whatever was the opposite of improving on what can be improved. That day she had made the effort. She gave them full marks for not bursting out laughing. At the end they said there were many applicants and her lack of experience might not stand her in excellent stead. She said she would set an example to show that make-up shouldn't be given too much credit and there were some problems with reference to appearances which it couldn't solve. 'People must keep their expectations in perspective' were the words she'd used, having come across them in *Vogue* magazine while waiting to see her doctor. They nodded sagely several times at that, more than they meant to in all probability. They didn't quite know whether she was taking the mickey.

They said they would tell her their decision in a letter. It was quite a nice letter, regretting etc. and wishing her good luck in her future career. She wrote back to thank them for giving her the time of day. She wished her letter had been more confident-looking. Her old typewriter, like everything else, had its limitations.

She wasn't ready to see her mother yet and it was a lovely day to walk the streets and keep to the shadows. Cleaning jobs were not without their interest. She wished there was a way of conveying that interest to her mother, who probably thought that cleaning was the best she could hope for.

Once, she witnessed a will. Or twice, to be accurate about it. It was in the general ward of a hospital. His name was Edgar Wakefield and they quite often had a chat. Except for his daughter late one afternoon, the only visitor he had was a woman who made a fuss of him, always patting his pillow and tidying his blankets and bringing him magazines. She leant over his bed, talking quietly to him. She gathered it was about his house, which was being kept tidy for him, and the garden. Or rather that was what he told her. 'One of those old-fashioned neighbours', he called her. Once she showed him some dirt under her fingernails, because she wanted him to know she was doing the weeding and it was a bad year for dandelions. Elsie couldn't get too close but she always tried to be there with her mop and bucket when the woman came, regular as the proverbial clockwork. Edgar told her how especially kind and 'thoughtful' she'd been ever since his wife had passed on. Her husband had also died, which gave them 'a fair amount in common'. He had a photograph of his wife in a silver frame which he kept by his bedside and often held face down on his chest. When the woman came he hid it away. There seemed something homely and smiling about her which was spoiled by her brisk fussiness and her smile that stayed the same.

One day the woman came with a smart-suited man who pulled the curtain round Edgar and about ten minutes later pulled it back very sharply. 'Might I prevail upon you to witness a signature?' he said with that superior voice people had when trying to show what perfect manners they had. Edgar signed the paper, then she signed it. The man looked around for someone else and the lady with the tea trolley happened to be passing, so she signed it too. The woman's smile did change then and never in her whole life had Elsie seen anyone look so pleased with themselves.

The next day Edgar told her he'd changed his will. There would still be a little left for his daughter. She lived a long way away, in Scotland, because her husband was in the off-shore oil industry. She'd only been to see her father once, staring at Elsie until she'd taken her mop and bucket well out of the way. 'We've never been close, and that's the honest truth,' Edgar told her afterwards. 'She can't get away from that family of hers, all the way from Aberdeen. Four grandchildren.

Two of them I've never even seen. They look good kids from the photos.'

For a week after that he was worried and not so chatty. He told her he'd fallen out with his daughter over an argument about how she behaved before she settled down. He said he saw now how he had been in the wrong. Who cared any longer about coloured hair and face-studs and short skirts and a drop too much drink on Saturday night, even pinching the odd car for a little spin? She was a 'reformed character now with kids and that'. It was Elsie's chief pleasure in life that people did sometimes like talking to her, almost as freely as talking to themselves. Then he asked her opinion. Had he done the right thing? He already knew he hadn't or he wouldn't have asked. The woman had stopped coming every afternoon. Elsie knew she imagined too much for her own good, guessing about people, dreaming up other worlds. But the bunches of grapes seemed to get smaller and the magazines looked as though they had passed through several hands. Perhaps she'd pilfered them from her doctor's waiting room. So in the end she'd typed a new will for him, just saying he wanted his daughter to have everything, giving Mrs Betty Stiles two thousand pounds for her trouble. She witnessed that will too with one of the nurses and took it to his bank with a letter saying it should be opened when he died. He put a finger to his lips and gave a big smile when he handed over the envelope.

It was very nice to be trusted, making you feel it was the only thing that mattered. If she hadn't been ugly and sort of neutral-looking and not expecting anything of life, Edgar's will might never have been changed at all. Before she went to sleep she sometimes thought of those grandchildren in years to come, going to university and starting to buy houses and driving around in nice cars and not knowing who they had to thank for that. If she found them and told them straight to their faces about their grandfather's will, they would be less thankful to him and not thankful to her because of the way she looked and might not enjoy their university education and other things so much. She just liked to think of them being more contented with life because of her, complete strangers to each other. These thoughts let her forget the children's mother, who wouldn't come near her father's bed until she was well out of the way. She often remembered the smile on Edgar's face when he gave her the envelope. She wished she could tell her mother of some of the kind things she'd done in her life. She wished she could call on old Edgar Wakefield for a character reference.

The sun had gone in and she made her way back into her mother's street. It was all in shadow now. She always looked first to see if the wedding photograph was lying on the desk. He'd walked out not long after she was born. She'd once overheard her mother say that it might have been the sight of his daughter that had driven him away. Geoffrey was ten by then. He was ashamed of her too but was always kind, not only when nobody else was there. Unless her imagination was running away with her again, it mightn't have been her their father couldn't stand the sight of. It might have been their mother. Anyway, he'd found another woman. No woman would want to blame herself for her husband walking out on her. So an ugly daughter might have been a convenience.

Her mother could hear people coming because of the crunch on the gravel. Once she said, 'It's not my usual postman today' when he was hardly through the gate. And she always said, 'I heard you coming.' Once she tried to take longer strides and on another day tiptoed as quietly as she could. But she said exactly the same thing. Like Edgar Wakefield's daughter, Geoffrey lived a long way away. Her mother told her more than once she didn't care for the kind of woman he'd married. Even her mother liked to tell her things. Once day his wife was 'hoity toity'. Another day she was 'common'. Elsie did not point out that she could hardly be both. She wasn't expected to express opinions. If she did she would tell her mother that it might have been Geoffrey's wife not liking her that had started it.

She couldn't stop wondering again if her mother's fatty wrinkled neck would make it harder to strangle her. Thinking about the noises she'd make would spoil her imagining Edgar Wakefield's grandchildren being handed their degrees at one of the leading universities, wearing those gowns and flat black hats with tassels. Edgar Wakefield's will had also made her think of strangling her mother, because of the money she would get from that. She wouldn't enjoy receiving a penny if every time she bought something she heard the sound of her mother gurgling her last. She wouldn't have to imagine that if someone else did it, like that man she met on the bus. Or not so often. Where did these horrid, horrid thoughts come from? If only her mother wouldn't rest her head back like that, showing so much of her neck... The gurgling and the sound of footsteps on a gravelled path...

She opened the gate and almost went away, unable to bring herself to tread on that gravel. There was so much more to her life than thoughts like that and cleaning jobs. From her room in Willesden she could look out in the spring and see four gardens away the flowering of a magnolia tree and soon after that a laburnum. In the other direction was a single tall silver birch tree that on a windy day tossed and swayed like a dancer. Soon after moving into her flat, she bought a book about trees and shrubs so she could enjoy other people's gardens. She would never have one of her own, not until her mother died. Her mother's garden wasn't big enough for trees. When she looked at them it was as if she was trying to change the subject of her life. They were beautiful. She watched gardening pro-grammes for the same reason.

Beauty was funny. She had begun taking a train or

a bus to visit those country houses with lovely gardens. She had joined the National Trust. Last Saturday she had sat on a white bench and watched the bumble-bees in a long line of lavender bushes, flitting quickly from flower to flower as if they weren't quite sure what they were looking for. Dissatisfied. They weren't there when the wind blew and then they returned. Still in a hurry, like shoppers. She picked a stalk of lavender and crumpled it in her hand and held it to her nose for a long time. A pair of women passing by looked worried that she might have a nosebleed. But they did not linger.

In those beautiful gardens people looked at her differently. Some did smile. This was for two reasons. About half were simply glad to see her there, able to enjoy herself looking at lovely things, forgetting herself, gardens bringing joy and escape to all and sundry without exception. The other half smiled as they would at anyone sharing their pleasure, with no further thoughts on the matter. On consideration, there weren't nearly so many of these, who didn't go on to feel sorry for her, who were pleased with themselves for having a shot at cheering her up. The majority looked at her very quickly as if she was so at odds with the beauty of it all that she shouldn't be there at all. They glanced away very quickly, especially in gardens with so much beauty to behold all around them. She wasn't what they wanted to remember when the day was over and they were sitting in their armchairs sipping whatever they sipped, the people who visited National Trust gardens, recalling the day they spent surrounded by so many varieties of shape and colour, and not mentioning that creature they saw gazing at the lavender. At least she set up a contrast for them, making the garden even more beautiful. She couldn't be sure if people thought like that.

One afternoon she saw a dead squirrel in a garden with ants swarming all over it and some bluebottles too. She couldn't help remembering that for a long time afterwards, even though it was a day when the rhododendrons were at their height. She couldn't think of anything more likely to obliterate the memory of a dead squirrel than that. She tried to keep a low profile when visiting gardens. She didn't sit in the café, though she might sneak round the edge of a kiosk and buy an ice-cream cone when there wasn't a queue. Not spoiling the pleasure for others was the least she could do when she wasn't making a major contribution to life in other respects.

Her mother's first words were, 'I heard you coming.' It was what she had dreaded, but then she added, 'I always say that, don't I? Boring of me.' She tried so hard to be natural that day, not moving around so much, not going back to the kitchen unnecessarily and turning on the telly. As always, she couldn't quite fathom her mother's expression. There might even have been love there but it looked like shame too. And, as always, she thought: 'Does she sometimes think I ought never to have been born? For my sake. The unhappiness it has caused me by being so ugly?' She longed more than anything to tell her mother that she shouldn't think like that.

That day she didn't mention her leg once. Elsie told her about the National Trust garden she had visited where she had watched the bees in the lavender. And her mother gave her five hundred pounds, saying she must visit those gardens as often as she liked. When she left there was a man on the bench at the bus stop hiding his face behind a newspaper. It was the sharply creased trousers and polished shoes that made her wonder if it was the man she had met on the bus. She should never have said that silly thing about killing her mother. And that cheque for five hundred pounds! And telling her to spoil herself a little. There wasn't any room for more things in her little flat. She had all the things she really needed. Her mother had been astonished at first when she'd told her she'd become a member of the National Trust. A look of happiness had crossed her face. As if at last her daughter had acquired a purpose in life. 'It doesn't matter what you look like in a beautiful garden,' she'd said to her mother. It was as if the shame had left her mother's eyes, no longer wondering if it would have been better if she had never been born.

At the end, she asked the question she had asked her father four years ago, the only time she had seen him.

'Why did our father leave us? Was it because of me?'

Her mother looked at her for longer than she ever had before. It was as if she was the one who was waiting for a reply, though she had always had it ready. She was listening for the sound of her own words.

'No, it wasn't because of you, Elsie. He found someone he liked more.'

'Someone without any children?'

'Yes.'

'Would he have been looking for her anyway?'

'I think he probably would.'

'What was wrong with you?'

But she only shrugged and gave half a smile and went out into the kitchen, though she had no need to. Elsie folded the cheque and put it into her purse. She had never loved her mother as she did at that moment.

III

THERE WAS THIS stupid fucking ugly cow on the bus. Kept on looking at him like she expected conversation. To shut her up, he told her he was just out of the nick for killing someone. She wanted the conversation so badly she told him she sometimes wanted to kill her mother. 'That'll be ten thousand quid,' he didn't reply. Just told her to fuck off. If he looked like an ex-con, it was because he was. It was true too he'd topped some-one. He ought to get an open-air job in the municipal gardens to put some colour in his cheeks. In that godawful warehouse there was no natural light at all. The levers of the fork-lift truck gave him backache. Looking his best, whatever that was now, or different anyway, wasn't a bloody option. He didn't see himself with a spade or fork in his hand, or raking up sodding dead leaves. He wished his thinking hadn't got so used to those words his mother hated – fucking this and sodding that. Perhaps one day he could change back to what he once was when she'd been proud of him and told him not to mix with people who didn't watch their language, like they couldn't have proper thoughts of their own.

He did follow the ugly cow. He didn't know why. Yes, he did. He had nothing else to do. He'd started wondering what sort of life a freak like that might have. Just being curious felt like something to live for. Must have scared the daylights out of her. She kept on looking round to see if he was following her. He crossed the street where people were milling about in front of the shop so she didn't see him. Being short with duck's disease, her walk was a sort of dumpy waddle. She kept to the shadows. When she reached the house he had to crouch behind a car because she turned so suddenly. He heard the crunch of her footsteps on the gravel. She wasn't there long and he sat on the bench at the bus stop. When she left, he'd have said she was upset but with a face like that you couldn't really tell. She was in a hurry as if the gravel was hot coals. Perhaps she's done her mother in herself so she wouldn't be needing him after all. Then the woman came out – more crunching of the gravel. She crossed the street towards the bus stop so he got a good look at her. She had that strict, cross look that old women sometimes had. Used to getting her own way. With a daughter like that, no bloody wonder.

He got in round the back, no problem, and

pinched fifty quid from a handbag that was just lying there. That plus some silver stuff which would fetch the odd bob: a wedding photo in a silver frame, a couple of candlesticks, cruet, sugar bowl. Nothing she couldn't afford, to judge from the new digital telly and furnishing generally. Red velvet curtains usually gave the show away. People like that had whole stacks of wedding photos in leather albums as often as not, so she'd only have to get another frame...

Since he came out he'd done a few jobs with Frank whom he'd met inside. He wasn't ever a thief. That was what the nick did for you. You lost your pride – us and sod the lot of them. There wasn't the sense of right and wrong any longer. From the very beginning his mother had told him, 'Just remember this. There's right and there's wrong.' Frank phoned as soon as he came out and he'd thought, why the fuck not? Who was he, anyway? Ex-con murderer. Scum. Trash. The usual. It was letting his mum down, that was all. He'd stop it one day. There was still some of Badger's money left. There was what they call the buzz. After fifteen years inside, what you wanted was buzz. Frank was the only one there he'd really got on with. Bloody cockney. Never stopped talking. He'd only do jobs like that when the spirit moved him. Frank never talked about what he was in for. 'You'll be performing a public service, Stanley,' Badger had told him. Frank would have a good laugh at that.

The rest couldn't give a toss about him, keeping

to himself the way he did, keeping his head down. They couldn't be bothered with him. Until he met Frank he couldn't be much bothered with himself. He'd have nothing to do with drugs. When his mother came to see him and said goodbye she sometimes added, 'Now don't you get into any trouble, Stan. You meet some bad types in places like this.' It was exactly the way she'd spoken to him when he was a boy.

He could see Badger Brandon now behind the table in the room at the Admiral Nelson, his cheeks puffed out as if he was going to vomit. He could hear that imitation-toff voice and the long words he used like it was yesterday. He could see the jewels in the rings on his fingers resting on his stomach and the gold tie-pin.

'I have received favourable reports of you, young Stanley,' he said very slowly in hardly more than a whisper.

He hadn't done anything. Just driven a van to France to do a favour for a mate. No idea what was in the packages they'd brought back. Then doing it again and each time getting five hundred quid in a smart white envelope. So he'd said nothing.

'Sit ye down, make yourself comfortable.'

The man standing behind him pulled out a chair with half a bow as though he was some sort of VIP. Badger lit a cigar, sucking on it and blowing out smoke between sentences. His cheeks hollowed and puffed out like a balloon being blown up. He was asking if by any remote chance he happened to have heard of the Boyd brothers, Ginger and Johnny. He'd nodded. There'd been talk about a turf war on the other side of town. A body had been found. A couple of stabbings.

'Well, Stanley, my friend, to cut a long story short, I have begun to find the Boyd brothers surplus to requirements, especially Ginger.'

The man reached into his pocket and laid a gun on the table. He'd begun shaking his head. He wanted to say he could never do a thing like that and began, 'I'm sorry, Mr Brandon, I...'

Badger raised his hands and moved his fingers as if to make the rings flash. There was no whisper in his voice now. 'Regard it in this fashion, Stanley. You'd be performing a public service.' He'd tried to interrupt, causing Badger to raise his hand. 'You see, Stanley, the way I understand it is this. You're an unknown quantity. And another matter to be considered is the benefit to your good self. Fifteen thousand. I've heard you have a delightful mother. You could spoil her a little.' The hands stopped moving but remained in the air like a surrender. He put down the cigar. 'I'd like you to do that for me, Stanley, you know, I really would.'

He was still shaking his head. The man pushed the gun towards him.

The long words had gone. Badger was staring at him. 'Follow instructions. Time and place. Do you comprehend me, Stanley?'

He'd nodded. Badger stood up. 'We'll be in touch.'

He offered his hand, nobbly with all those rings.

He'd never forget that final smile, the gleaming white teeth like an advertisement, and his eyes. They weren't harsh or cruel. They were amused, almost gentle. 'You're a good lad, Stanley. I hope you are fully aware of that.'

Finally, Badger lifted the gun off the table and put it in Stan's pocket, patting it as if it was a gift.

It was getting dark in the car park. Ginger had been summoned there, expecting to settle some deal. He was arrested four days later. He hadn't even got rid of the gun. While he was on remand, he'd heard that Badger had called him a bloody silly little fool. But he'd been as good as his word about the money...

He could never get out of his mind Johnny Boyd drawing his hand across his throat as he left the court that day. And the note he was given a week before they let him out. Enjoy it while you can, you bastard. He hoped it would be quick. If it wasn't for his mother he sometimes thought it would be good fucking riddance, a good-for-nothing coward like him.

They didn't know in the warehouse he was an ex-con. It was all in the north. Nor did the woman he'd bumped into two days after he'd come down to London. He did the odd thieving job so he could spoil her a bit. That was what he could tell himself. All he did was help Frank by driving his van. Looking out and that. Ten per cent wasn't bad. The thing about Frank was he was careful, a real pro, not in the big time any longer. 'Jewellery in Mayfair! Those were the days,' he said. 'And those were the days I did time for. Keep it simple, Stan, that's my advice.'

The woman had a little girl. Her father came to see them on the spur of the moment so he couldn't stay over too often. The sod had left her and all that, but still thought she was good for a screw for old times' sake. He didn't mind she had someone else. He just came in and sat there, waiting for his shag, until he left. Big bugger. 'See you,' Sherrill said as if he'd called by to read the electricity meter. When the coast was clear he could have been the only man in the world, the way she carried on.

He tried to give her a good time. The extra cash came in handy, she said, was there any more where that came from? He got forty quid for that silver frame, plus another hundred for the other silver stuff. She gave him a right going-over that evening. 'You can't say you don't get your money's worth,' she said. Her bloke came in very late, half pissed, so he left sharpish. Not much doubt he'd get his end away that night, telling him to take that fucking stupid grin of his face. She winked at him when he left. She wouldn't dare to do that normally.

He said a quiet word of thanks to that ugly bitch on the bus for giving him one of the best shags of his life. That was the sort of rotten way of thinking prison had taught him. Perhaps he'd bump into her again because it was a bus he often took back from the ware-house. Perhaps next time she'd offer him ten thousand quid to do in her mother. He might be a worthless sod but he'd never do a thing like that, not to someone who looked so bloody sad. Not to a stranger. Money wasn't everything, was it? So people went on telling him on those useless sodding rehabilitation courses. Mind you, if he looked half like that woman on the bus, he probably wouldn't have a lot of love in him at all. He might even talk to complete strangers, tell them he couldn't stand the sight of his mother.

When he went back to see his mother he'd never tell her he was doing a bit of thieving. His mum had a lovely heart. A bit on the simple side, to tell the truth. She'd never understand why anyone could have a thought like that. She didn't like the killing he did, ending up where he did all those years. But even she said it was good riddance, to make him feel better about himself. It was against her nature. That was what she told him, because he felt bad enough about himself already. It wasn't against her nature to want to make him feel better about himself. She never said 'I love you' like everyone else did these days. She didn't need to. She wouldn't have seen the point of it. He liked going to see her and watching television with her. It didn't matter what was on. She'd watch anything, even golf. Her trusty companion, she called it.

He didn't tell Frank about the photo frame and other silver stuff from that woman's house. A bit of freelance on the side wouldn't worry him. Let's be truthful about it: it did cross his mind to wonder what he'd have done if that evil-looking bitch had offered him fifty thousand to do her mother in. Easy to get in. They'd never catch him. There wouldn't be the connection. He imagined doing it and telling himself it served her bloody right for the way she treated her daughter. It only crossed his mind, that's all. You had thoughts. You couldn't help it when you didn't have the self-respect, they called it.

He didn't even look at Ginger's face after he put the bullet in his head. All he could remember was the perfect haircut he had and the fresh white collar of his shirt in the dying light as the car-park lamps came on. Fresh out of the wrapper, it could have been. It came back, not to haunt him exactly, but he wouldn't remember the back of an old woman's head, the neat curls after a visit to the hairdresser. An old woman. Of course he wouldn't. He wasn't being serious. A steady job and a bit of thieving for his woman and her little one suited him fine. With Ginger he didn't have the choice. He had it coming from someone. The thoughts went round and round, getting nowhere. He wouldn't expect them to, the stupid useless bastard he was, waiting for Johnny Boyd to catch up with him.

'Good riddance.' She only said that once so he could hardly hear her. When she came to visit she never asked about any of it, so he wouldn't have to think she wanted to judge him. He'd only said in the court he was guilty as charged. He didn't have to

38

tell her anything else. It would have been like asking
her to make up her mind about him when he was all
she had.

IV

SHE'D ONLY put the wedding photo on the desk in case
Elsie asked to see it. They were welcome to it. Ditto
the candlesticks and other stuff included in Henry's
calculations as part of her share of the estate. When did
she ever light candles? When had she ever? She'd rather
have the insurance money any day.

She'd almost enjoyed Elsie's visit this time.
Mentioning her father at last. If only all those years of
watchful motherhood hadn't tired the love out of her.
Perhaps some people were born with more love in
them than others. She must have said things she
shouldn't have said. Elsie should never have thought
that she was why Robert left her. He'd found another
woman he fancied more than her, that was all. That was
the long and short of it, if Elsie could believe that.
Better in bed, as simple as that. She'd met her twice.
Common as common but with one of those wobbly

bodies you couldn't help imagining, and lips open and pushed forward a bit, expecting a kiss. She'd never said to anyone, 'I don't know what Robert sees in her.'

Well, at least she had Geoffrey. If only he didn't live so far away and anyway, she and his Susan didn't like each other. She had no idea why. He'd stuck up for Elsie but being ten years older he didn't have to do it for long. He'd take her to the park or the shops. There were one or two who made ugly faces behind her back. Or just giggled… Of course, she'd made them feel lucky they weren't born like that. She'd made the girls feel prettier. Elsie had loved going out with Geoffrey. She became all excited and once wetted herself. She'd had that gurgling chuckle that made her look like some sort of lunatic. She wasn't that by a long chalk. Once or twice she had seen her laugh and smile at herself in the mirror, along with other expressions, but she had learnt to stop doing them. You could never guess what she was thinking. She used to read away in her bedroom for hours. She loved beautiful things, sometimes pointing out some flowers that other children would just think were boring. When Elsie came she made sure there were flowers in the house because she liked them so much. She always said how lovely they were, touching them as if to make sure they were real.

The day the wedding photo was stolen she went to see Gladys. There were the same old people there. They'd done the usual hand-holding but there weren't any spirits that day. No Arthur and his blessed geraniums.

There hardly ever were. They only 'had a go' for the so-called fun of it. Mostly they were there for the bridge. If there were too many of them, the spare women would knit or sew and join in the natter or they took turns. It should be nice having regular friends, asking each other about their loved ones. She'd told them Elsie had a good steady job, which she always did but not often the same one. And that was it. No mention of impending weddings or children or burdensome responsibilities. They spoke about their loved ones with great pride but there was tiredness in it too: from knowing them for so long, and for all the disappointments there were, the not living up to expectations. It was hard not to smile when you asked about so-and-so and before they replied there was always a sigh. Everyone had gone beyond them now and had their own lives to lead. You could hardly blame them for that. They weren't often in their loved ones' minds. And when they were, there were sighs to be imagined there too. They never asked about Elsie nowadays because, although they couldn't hear it, hers was the loudest sigh of all. Poor Elsie. If only she knew how much pity and restraint there was because of her. On second thoughts, she probably did. Her face never showed how much she hated or liked her, or didn't.

They knew how well off she was. The way they looked at her sometimes, you might think it was her fault she came into something when her father died. There were the comments about detached houses and driveways. Every time she heard that crunch on the gravel she'd think of their 'little group'. She made sure she pretended to be less good at bridge than she was, although she was better than the rest of them put together. She pretended to be scatterbrained, letting them tease her, but there wasn't the same jocularity in it as when they teased the others. There was much conversation about how dear things were these days, with glances in her direction, as if to say that that wouldn't matter so much to some. She could hardly not tell them she went on cruises from time to time, and they could see how often she had her hair done. That morning Ethel Wainwright had said she didn't think she and her husband could afford Torquay again this year, the way prices had gone through the roof. Her husband was an invalid. He probably wasn't as crippled as she would like them to think he was, 'slaving away' being one of her frequent expressions. They knew Dorothy's husband had left her. They'd all seen Elsie at one time or another. Elsie allowed them to feel sorry for her and therefore not mind so much that she was richer than they were.

She couldn't guess whether they thought she might have given Elsie more love and support. When she told them she went up the Nile for a week, Mary Crayshaw asked as casually as she could, while trumping a trick with that flourish and grunt of hers, whether she'd taken Elsie with her. 'Not this time,' she'd replied.

She did voluntary work where a kind of love was less uncertain. There were the three mornings a week in the Oxfam shop. She sold raffle tickets for Scope, and people could often see her outside Tesco's rattling some tin or other. She couldn't talk about that on their bridge afternoons because they would think she was boasting about what a good person she was and as far as she knew none of them did anything for charity at all. They had grandchildren and gardens (smaller than hers, they kept on reminding her, so not requiring a gardener), and couldn't consider themselves to be 'ladies of leisure by any stretch of the imagination.' They'd seen her in the charity shop and rattling her tins. 'Doing your good works again,' they might say. Or 'I'd love to have the time.' The day one of them actually said 'It's all right for some', she'd never go near their bridge club again. But she probably always would. She would be more lonely without it. Cruises weren't the same. Never setting eyes on people again, not if you could possibly help it, you often felt like adding. Liking people more than you would if you didn't have to. Sometimes she even heard her inner voice say, 'I hate these people.' But on the whole they were nice enough to her and made her feel welcome. It wouldn't have been the same if it hadn't been for Elsie.

When Gladys had one of her séances they drew the curtains and held hands and Gladys tried to bring in someone, usually Mavis's husband. In fact, it was always Mavis who asked her to have a go and it was always Arthur they had to ask for at some stage in the proceedings. To judge from the way Mavis talked about feeling Arthur's presence, Dorothy couldn't help thinking he jolly well ought to be able to see her geraniums for himself. Sometimes they put the letters of the alphabet in a circle with 'Yes' and 'No' at the top and bottom. Then they each put a finger on an upturned glass and Gladys asked, 'Is anyone there?' Once they got as far as the glass sliding to a 'Yes' and then spelling out the name 'Sidney'. But then the glass whizzed about from letter to letter and made no sense unless Sidney was Turkish or something. It was tiring after a while keeping one's finger on the glass. They had got a few other words, with spelling mistakes. The best so far was when a woman, or girl, called Kate said, 'My lovely garden.' But nobody knew anyone called Kate with or without an interest in gardens...

Still, it made a change, for all the disappointment. It was when they did Ouija that Dorothy found herself not liking them, the daft, intense looks on their faces and the little sighs and giggles. She imagined Elsie there, becoming less ugly in the darkened room. She entered into the spirit of it, wanting them to like her in spite of her detached house and superior riches. They must wonder why she didn't invite them to her house, or to sit in the garden in summer. They could go on wondering until the cows came home for all she cared.

It was the deep breathing when they tried to get into a trance that had begun to get on her nerves. Mavis had bronchial trouble, so from time to time the breathing was interrupted by a little rattle. Together they sounded puffed as if worried they wouldn't finish the course.

Gladys once persuaded Dorothy to try to get in touch with her father. 'Perhaps he knows Arthur,' she said. She could hear her father's loud, abrupt voice: 'What I suggest, Miss Nosey Parker, is that you mind your own damned business.'

When Gladys gave up trying, Dorothy said, 'Perhaps they'd rather we left them in peace.'

'Unless they don't want to be,' said Mabel who'd never tried to get in touch with anyone, who'd never seemed to want to, as though the dead would be just as much trouble as they had been in life.

There was a silence, with nothing left to talk about. Gladys resented what Dorothy had said. She twiddled her fingers to brush some crumbs off and said, 'And how is your Elsie these days?'

Dorothy reached down for her handbag, pretending not to have heard.

'I'll be off then,' she said. 'Not sure I can make it next week.'

Never again, she was thinking. Then she added, 'I shall be spending the day with my daughter. Perhaps I could bring her along too? She'd love to learn to play bridge and I could tell her she might be able to have a word with her grandfather. You will be able to see for yourselves how she is.'

There was no response to that except from Mavis, who began to say, 'That would be ni...' She heard her father's voice: 'Not if I have anything to do with it, she bloody won't.'

V

DEAR DOROTHY

I have to say I was a little surprised to receive your letter about the cottage, expressing disappointment that I was intending to sell it without your authority.

The plain fact of the matter is that when Father died, his inheritance was left to us equally and we agreed the cottage should be included in my share of his estate.

The fact that property prices have substantially increased over recent years is not a factor that can reasonably be taken into account. My solicitor advises me that the law is clear on the matter. Indeed, I remember clearly Father saying towards the end that the cottage would be a nice 'bolt-hole' for me and Pru, you yourself not seeming to have any great interest in the countryside.

I do accept that now Geoffrey has children of his

own, the cottage would be an asset for him too. Indeed, I have more than once let you know when it would be free for him to use it for a week or two, provided he gave us ample notice so that we could prepare it for him and his young family. The same would of course apply to Elsie, though I do not recall your ever asking me before to include her in the reckoning.

The plain fact of the matter is that we are now proceeding to put the cottage on the market. I regret it will no longer be available to you and yours but our decision is final, following our decision to purchase a little place in Spain. It is in a delightful new housing complex adjoining a golf course and only five miles from the sea where we intend to spend several months of the year, perhaps building up to more than that as the years pass. It of course goes without saying that we hope you will come and stay with us there on occasion. It might be more difficult to accommodate Geoffrey (or Elsie for that matter) unless, again, there was considerable notice, bearing in mind that we will let it from time to time, on strict conditions, I need hardly add, since it will be a fully furnished home from home and any temporary occupants will have to be carefully vetted.

I hope I have satisfactorily answered your letter. For Father's sake I apologise for the disappointment. These decisions are never easy. You will experience a similar wrench should you ever decide to leave the house you acquired from Father's estate where you have lived for so long, (and which has also appreciated very considerably in value).

Pru joins me in sending you my love. I do not expect to be in your part of the world in the foreseeable future but perhaps you would like to pay us another visit before too long.

Henry

That should put paid to all that, he thought. He agreed with Pru it was a 'bit of a cheek' Dorothy telling them she was 'disappointed' not to have been consulted about selling the cottage. Geoffrey had only asked to use it once and he'd had to be pretty firm in pointing out they needed a bit more notice, and anyway, that was the time they were having the central heating installed. He never asked again. Poor little Elsie asked once too, phoning out of the blue. At first he hadn't recognised her cockneyfied accent, and she had to say, 'It's your niece Elsie, Uncle Henry. Don't you remember me?' He'd hesitated a bit and had to make up his mind pretty sharpish when she'd said she would like to stay there for a long weekend with a couple of friends she worked with in a school kitchen. He thought it was 'school'. 'They are very respectable, Uncle Henry,' she'd said. 'We'll leave the place spotless. You won't even know we've been there.' He'd still hesitated and then she'd said of course they'd pay him a proper rent.

He'd said he'd call her back. Pru told him she'd have none of it. She'd first met Elsie when he took her to meet Dorothy in their father's house. He'd frankly been very surprised by Pru's behaviour that day. Normally hard to please, and that was putting it mildly, he'd never known her so charming. He'd warned her what to expect. They'd gone for a walk on the common and Pru went ahead with Elsie so that he could have a chat with Dorothy about family matters: there was some silver she had no use for, but he'd told her to keep it. Anyway, Elsie took Pru's hand and they ran ahead and he could hear their laughter as they got caught in the middle of a football game. Elsie had tried to kick the ball and fallen over. The boys had stared at her as she lay there with her legs in the air, trying to roll over to get up. You could see how disgusted they were as Pru helped Elsie to her feet and the boys slinked off, muttering and giggling. He'd been very proud of Pru that day, not least because Dorothy was so happy to see Elsie enjoying herself for a change. At tea afterwards Elsie just sat forward and tried to drink her tea daintily with her little finger sticking up and hardly answering Pru's questions about her school. Elsie seemed to have stopped enjoying herself. The fun was over. But it was impossible to tell what Elsie was thinking, the way she moved her face as little as possible, and her eyes so overshadowed by her brow it was difficult to see them. Dorothy didn't try to help her with the questions about her school, in fact, hardly looked at her. It was easy to tell she was in a hurry for them to go, to spare them the strain of having to be with Elsie a moment longer than they had to. But Pru had persisted and finally persuaded Elsie to take her up to her room to see all the books she had.

On the way back he'd said to Pru what a strain it must have been bringing Elsie up, the looks she must have got, the teasing at school, the lack of boyfriends, indeed friends of any kind, the absence of hope that one day she would have a family of her own. He'd gone on a bit like that, saying it wasn't as if she was handi-capped, when people would rally round and so on. She was just stunted, if that was the word, and her face – he'd never use the word out loud and he didn't to Pru, not then or at any other time – was just very ugly: the deep-set eyes close together, squinting slightly, hardly any lips, those big protruding teeth, big chin with two hairy moles and tight, curly light brown hair. And that sort of moist, rough voice as though her tongue was too big. Well, he'd said it out loud, not all of it but more than he meant to. In the end, after a long silence, Pru had said, 'Well, that's Elsie summed up for you.'

When Elsie came to stay, Pru did her stuff and took her out shopping. On the one occasion he'd accompanied them she'd said very sharply to a group of lads, 'What do you think you're staring at?' This made Elsie blush, so it perhaps wasn't as kind as it sounded. Anyway, it had surprised him a bit when Pru had put her foot down about Elsie going to stay at the cottage with her friends. What she said was: 'I don't want ever to have any reason to stop liking her and feeling sorry for her.' Which was too deep for him.

He regretted the tone of his letter as soon as he'd sent it. After all, Elsie was his niece and blood was thicker, they said. He was only a simple quantity surveyor and didn't know anything about genes and such like. Elsie probably got the way she looked from that Flash Harry father of hers. That crinkly hair and big chin. Ghastly man. Loud was the word for it. Not only his voice, boasting of this and that. Smoking a pipe to give himself a touch of class and then ditching Dorothy for some tart as soon as he saw how Elsie would turn out. He'd always told Dorothy to have nothing to do with him – he was after her money etc. It was a mercy Pru had never met him. He would have made a pass at her. There were some types she couldn't stand. The life in Spain, she couldn't wait until she felt too old for it. Her the swimming. Him the golf. She did say once they could have Elsie to stay, a real treat it would be. But she'd stand out more in those surroundings, with that stale-looking complexion of hers like old bread and everyone there trying to look so well preserved and healthy-looking. Admittedly, it was the sort of place where you'd be likely to come across more than a few of those Flash Harrys like Dorothy's ex, always putting their arms round you.

It had been decidedly odd, the way that Pru had taken to Elsie. There was that side to her. Putting a finger up to the world. Showing she was different and couldn't care less. She wasn't exactly the woman he wanted her to be. The finger she put up was also to him, especially that day with Elsie. She'd shown him up rather, setting an example. Whose niece was she? That was it. She probably liked Elsie because she didn't seem to like anyone else much, himself included, come to think of it. Come to think of it too, it was probably quite a good thing, in fact, a jolly good thing, they didn't have their own children, all the argy-bargy that would have led to.

VI

THEY HARDLY ever talked about Elsie, Geoffrey realised. Why should they? Susan would see no reason to, except when the presents arrived for the twins and thank-you letters had to be written. They had a picture of their aunt in their minds as someone very rich and glamorous and famous. There seemed no harm in let-ting them go on believing that. After hearing about the cottage, Geoffrey reminded Susan he'd only asked Uncle Henry once if they could spend a week there and he'd been 'bloody pompous about it, actually'.

'I gather from Mum,' he added, 'that Elsie asked him if she could take some friends there.'

He'd told her that already. Her back was turned to him and she was arranging flowers in a vase. Suddenly she became still.

'Never again, he can stuff his cottage,' he went on, more quietly. He just wanted her to say something.

'He was very apologetic about it, Mum said.'

She put the vase down on the table right in front of him. She seemed fed up: having to say something about Elsie, was it? Or because she'd said more than once the cottage would be lovely to take the children to if he hadn't been so stubborn about asking? But her question was about Elsie.

'I bet he was. Anyway, how is Elsie these days?'

She went out into the kitchen, hardly waiting for a reply, so he had to raise his voice.

'Mum says she's got quite a good job. She visits gardens and things at weekends.'

'What sort of a job?' she called back.

'Not sure. Cleaning, I think.'

Then she did come back and sat opposite him at the table, the flowers between them.

There was a pause. 'Must try and see Elsie when I'm next in London,' he said.

'Oh come! You never go to London.'

She had spoken sharply, as if wanting to shame him.

'Well, what about inviting her up here then?' he said, trying to get his own back a bit. 'What about Christmas?'

She stood up abruptly, moving the vase carefully to one side. 'You know what we're both thinking. The effect on the kids... How they'd cope... and so on...'

She turned back towards the kitchen. Her hands were in front of her as if still holding the flowers.

'And so on...' he said too loudly. 'Let's think about it.' He had to call after her again. 'Any day now the birthday presents will turn up.'

Susan came back and stared down at him. 'I do wish she wouldn't. I really do. They think she's some beautiful Fairy Godmother.'

He could not look back at her. The shame hadn't gone away. 'We're all the family she's got,' he muttered. Think of it like that.'

Susan shrugged and went up the stairs.

Geoffrey sat there, thinking about Uncle Henry and that Pru woman of his. 'Another time, old chap,' he'd drawled about the cottage. Another time his arse. He could easily have phoned and said when it would be available. As for Elsie, 'he wouldn't want her to make a habit of it', his mother had said. 'On her own perhaps, but "friends", dear me!' She imitated Uncle Henry's voice quite well, he had to admit.

Why did she dislike her brother so much? Their father's favourite? Something about his will. Perhaps he just wasn't a very nice man. A lot of people weren't, as it happened. He'd been pleasant enough to Susan, chatting her up as if he wasn't there. Aunt Pru made her impatience quite clear: 'We do have to get on, Henry.' She'd treated Susan like a dowdy housewife, not actually saying she should try to get out and about a bit. Susan thought she was frightful, that they both were. There was no need to go on about that. Sell the cottage. Good riddance. He couldn't think of a single reason why they need ever see Uncle Henry again.

Of course it was Elsie he ought to see. Once, just before he left home, she'd got a bit carried away and said, 'You're the best thing in my whole life.' Mum used to say, very simply, 'She loves you, you know. You know how to make her happy.' But he was a lot older and left home and that was that

He'd last seen her a year ago. He'd gone to her little flat. She had made it look very nice with floral curtains and furniture. It was spotless. She had poured him a glass of sweet sherry and her hand was shaking when she handed him the little dishes of olives and nuts she'd prepared. She'd rather bubbled over, trying to make her work sound interesting and showing him all that bumf about the National Trust. One of its houses was near Uncle Henry's cottage and he'd made some comment about how nice it would be to stay there for the odd weekend. Something like that. 'Ooh yes!' she'd said as if she was expecting him to arrange it. She'd said that Uncle Henry had been so kind when she'd plucked up the courage to phone him about it. She had lovely friends at the hospital, she'd explained. They'd really look after it. After all, they did work in a hospital where cleanliness ought to be everything. She did ramble on a bit in that clogged voice of hers. When he'd got up to go, she'd given him a very clumsy, very hasty embrace and he'd remembered the day when she'd told him he was 'the best thing in the world'.

Susan was right: he only went to London once in

a blue moon. He'd told her about the visit to see Elsie but she hadn't said anything. After they'd met Elsie at their mother's to tell her of their engagement, Susan had said, 'You can't tell anything from that face, the features have taken away all expressiveness from it. There was something in her eyes that might have been jealousy or might have been joy'. Since then, Susan had said next to nothing else about Elsie, as if that had just about said it all. Now it was only when the thank-you letters had to be written. To be fair, she had so many other things on her mind. The twins. Trying to hold down that sales job. Umpteen things, including him. And frankly, there wasn't an awful lot about Elsie you could say. She was just there somewhere. His poor sister. He wished he didn't mean so much to her. He wished she had someone else to give her affection to. He wished she didn't send those presents. At least she had her mother. He wished he knew how much love there was between them, if there was any at all.

He hadn't told Elsie, or their mother, for that matter, that their father had once written to say he'd like to keep in touch from time to time. He'd nearly phoned him to tell him to get stuffed, but in the end simply didn't bother to reply. What did Elsie think about him? He wished he knew that too.

VII

WHEN ELSIE had first seen the wedding photograph four years ago, she hadn't been able to stop wondering how he might have changed since then. Why had her mother put it there face down on the desk? It was as if he was peering out at her, saying 'Here I am.' His smile was crooked, as if worried that he might be smiling too much. He had his arm round her mother but she wasn't smiling. It was funny that that was the photo they'd chosen to put in the silver frame. They were alone with the church in the background. They had a sort of deserted look as if they were waiting for the guests to turn up. Her father was wearing a very colourful tie which might have been flowery. There were flowers around the entrance to the church, red and mauve rhododendrons. Her father's buttonhole was red too. His look changed to one of eagerness, that they should try to love each other, as if he didn't know what lay in store for him. In that instant she felt sorry for him. Her mother in her white dress, with her white bouquet, was so small beside him, helpless almost, as if to say that it wasn't her idea to be taking photographs. It would be storing up memories. Elsie closed her eyes and whispered she was sorry for letting them down.

Her mother had come in with a fresh teapot. At first she said nothing but as Elsie was leaving, she gave her an extra squeeze and said, 'He looked quite dashing, didn't he? He had his choice of the ladies.'

After that, Elsie could never tell her she'd been to see him.

He lived by the seaside. She did not want him to die before she saw him again. He might want to see her too, for a final word before the curtain came down on his life. She didn't want him lying there at the end like Edgar Wakefield with regrets in his heart. He could always tell her just to go away, please, and leave them in peace, bygones were bygones etc. If it was still the two of them.

She walked to the sea from the station. It was a lovely day with wind blowing up the waves to make them flash and sparkle and sweeping across them in sudden gusts like swarms of insects. The gulls were blown this way and that above the harbour where fishing boats were coming in. There was a bench with an old man alone on it, but he left as soon as she sat down, after one glance at her. It didn't matter who she was. She was just someone else to disturb his remembering.

Out there over the horizon there were worlds after worlds, there were jungles and ice floes and deserts and mountains. There were two ships on the horizon which seemed not to be moving. How could she be so content with her father only a few minutes walk away, a father she had only seen in a photograph? It was knowing that she would be doing her duty. She did not want to try to love him. She did not want him lying there at the end, wishing he had said something to his only daughter. The sea was so dazzling and alive and endless. There were so many places to sit and watch the world, like bumble-bees in a long row of lavender. And that magnolia tree four gardens away from her flat, followed by the laburnum in the garden beyond that, and the tall silver birch swaying like a dancer.

The bungalow was freshly decorated, the cement between the red bricks painted white, and a glossy door blue like the sea. The tiles were like choppy dark red waves. There were five shrubs surrounded by wood chippings to keep away the weeds: two azaleas, a rose of Sharon, a crocosmia and a snowberry. Along the bed under the window was a row of freshly pruned roses. The bird bath had been filled with fresh water and there were two little bird houses with trays for the seed. It was in the middle of a row of other bungalows which she'd walked past. All the gardens were neat like that. Two had rockeries, which made a change and allowed the growing of more exotic plants. She always liked those in the National Trust gardens: the little heathers and rock plants pushing out from between the stones.

On the gate of her father's bungalow was a name: Traveller's Rest. She didn't know what travelling her father had ever done. Perhaps it had always been called that and it might be bad luck to change the name of a house. It wasn't what she'd expected after her mother's house with its high hedges, from which you couldn't see other houses except from upstairs. She'd imagined her father in all sorts of ways. She'd seen him with a rakish, nautical hat, steering a ship, smoking a cigar in an expensive black car, even riding a horse in a show-jumping competition. He had always had a big house and garden, much bigger than her mother's, in which the National Trust might have expressed an interest. In her dreams there were large dogs romping on lawns, and croquet, and stables. And the rooms were high-ceilinged with chandeliers and broad staircases. The dreams came and went. She had to place him somewhere in her mind. She tried not to make him ridiculous, with servants running round after him and leading the chase of foxes and organising fêtes in his grounds. She had invented worlds for him where she would have been in the way and caused embarrassment. She had imagined hiding behind hedges to watch the dancing on the lawn, or peering through the banisters at the arrival of guests for the annual winter ball. At first, when she was a child and had these dreams of him, she would follow him round and he would introduce her as she handed round peanuts and olives. But soon the dreams became darker, the lawns were more often in shadow and the chandeliers did not light up the stairs and she became invisible. She could not hate him for his shame of her. It was such a beautiful world he lived in, which he had made himself. It wasn't his fault that she did not belong there, that she had ever been born.

She knocked on the door and soon it opened. An old woman with a small white face covered her mouth and gasped. Her eyes stared out as though at something that was falling from the skies.

'I'm sorry,' she said. 'It's Elsie. I've only come to see my father.'

The woman gasped again behind both hands now and hurried away, calling out, 'Robert! Robert! You'd better come. It's for you.'

A door slammed and then after a long pause an old man appeared from a room at the end of the hall. He moved very slowly with a limp and had a stick. He leant forward, peering towards her as though he had forgotten his glasses.

She was in the shadow of the door and he came close to her. 'Who is it? Who is it?' He cleared his throat and said it again, 'Who is it?'

She moved out of the shadow and said, 'I'm very sorry, Father. I hope I haven't come at an inconvenient time.'

'Oh my dear God!' he said, turning sideways,

ready to shuffle off if there hadn't been a coat-rack in the way. She heard the sound of something being smashed in the room where the woman had gone. Her father backed away down the hall. He didn't seem to need his stick any longer. She hadn't expected him to be so old. He was bald and his eyebrows were very bushy, almost joining the tufts of hair in front of his ears. His nose was pink like the patches on his cheeks. His eyes had stared at her. They were not the same as the eyes in the photograph. They seemed to have whitened and to have become afraid. They were trying not to be angry. They were like the eyes of the murderer she had met on the bus.

'Look, I don't want to…' he began.

He sidled back to the room where the woman had gone and closed the door, but not before she heard the woman say, 'Just get her out of here, Robert! The past is the past. What the hell does she want?' Her voice was squeaky as if someone had her by the throat. Elsie wanted to go in there to say again how very sorry she was. For she was sorry. She had only wanted to hear any final words her father might have for her. Standing there in the open doorway, she wondered if that was the last she would see of them, if her father had nothing to say to her at all. He would not lie there in his hospital, fretting about things unspoken. Perhaps it would be better if she went back to look at the wind stirring up the sea.

Her father moved slowly towards her.

'You'd better come along in,' he said, leading her back to the room at the end of the corridor. It was a room with much floral decoration covering the curtains and carpets. There were too many colours. There were too many ornaments too: vases, and little statues of people and animals, and pots and saucers. There were even two china horses prancing on the television set. Two of the pictures on the walls were of gardens which probably belonged to the National Trust. The third picture was of a swarthy lady in what might have been Spanish costume. There was also a flower in her hair, a red camellia it might have been. In the background was a masted ship and a flat, very blue sea. Her father was pointing to a chair. It faced a French window beyond which she could see a lawn and a garden-shed. She wanted to save him any more embarrassment.

'I won't have tea or coffee, thank you very much' she said. 'There was a nice café at the railway station.'

She spoke very clearly and politely. She wanted him to know that, whatever else she was, she had turned out to be a well-mannered person he need not be ashamed of, and in the time left to him that might be a consolation. She had dressed as nicely as she could in a tweed suit and blouse, not knowing what she would find there. He had no choice, sitting there opposite her but to see her as she was. Perhaps the light from the French window made her indistinct. There was clattering in the room where the woman had gone, which made him shake his head.

'Well, Elsie,' he began, shifting to make himself more comfortable. She sat very upright with her hands resting on her knees. He was staring hard at her now, forcing himself to, perhaps.

'To what do I owe this honour?' he continued.

'I thought you might wish to see me. It was in case you did, I mean.'

He paused to rub his knees and winced, indicating pain there. 'Well yes, to be honest, I did wonder. Of course I did. I received a letter, a short letter from your mother, some three, four years ago, to tell me you were out in the world; "self-sufficient", I think her word was.'

'Why did you leave her?' she asked. 'That is what has been on my mind from time to time.'

'Ah well, that's rather long ago, isn't it?' He cleared his throat laying a hand on his chest to show there was something wrong there too, that he was not in a proper state of health to be upset by anything sudden or unsettling. There was a further clattering, reminding sound from the other room. 'There's nothing unusual about it, is there? Not these days. People move on.'

She sat even more upright, putting one hand on top of the other, slightly clenched. She didn't want to appear as if she was accusing him of something. He might feel more relaxed if he could take those pale eyes off her for a moment. There were so many objects for his glance to roam over, to give himself a casual air. Perhaps he thought he'd said everything that needed to be said. He even leant forward as if about to stand up and say 'Will that be all, then? It's been nice meeting you again. Thank you for taking the trouble.' He cleared his throat again, putting his hand round it. What he said was, 'As you can see, we live quite modestly. It's scrimping and saving time. Had to give up work early. Not enough put aside. We'd wanted another dog but they're such an expense, and then having to walk it with my arthritis...'

She had come for money – it wouldn't have been worth the journey otherwise. All that way from London. Were those the thoughts running through his head? Was he thinking: her mother has got more than enough. What does she want from me? She didn't want him to have those questions in his mind. Not when he was receiving a visit from his daughter after all these years and there was little time left for him. When she might ease his conscience and he could die in peace.

'Was it because I am very ugly that you left us?'

One hand went to his breast, the other to his throat. 'Oh no, Elsie, you mustn't ever think that. Please don't think that. Really...'

'It was because you met another woman whom you preferred in certain ways to our mother.'

There was another clattering sound from the kitchen, another jogging of his memory. He did not want to reply.

'It was so long ago. These things are happening all the time. They are outside our management... Happenings, choices. I was never a deep man, good at analysing and the rest of that caboodle.'

'You didn't want to keep in touch with Geoffrey either?'

'We thought, she thought, it should be a completely fresh start. When life moves on, you have to move with it. I did write to Geoffrey but...'

There was a pause. His mouth was still open. The woman had come in and stood behind Elsie. Out of the corner of her eye, Elsie could see there was a tea towel wrapped around her hands like manacles.

'Come along now!' she said. 'There's no point raking over the coals. No point at all. It was kind of you to call, I'm sure. Leave sleeping dogs alone... Come along, Robert. Or have you forgotten you have a doctor's appointment?'

He sat up, as if to attention. 'Of course, dear, of course.' He began to get up.

Elsie turned enough for the woman to see her again, full in the face. Her complexion was less white now. There must have been cream on it when she opened the door. She had become younger; her hair flowed more freely about her head, blonde, not grey, as if in that brief time she had given herself a colour shampoo. The woman watched her father get to his feet. Elsie stood up and went to help him.

The woman tried to stop herself from shouting,

'It's better for him all round to do things for himself, not treat him like an invalid.'

Elsie went on helping him and he grunted his thanks. The woman left, making a 'tsk' sound.

When she was out of earshot, he whispered, 'Thank you, Elsie. Thank you for doing that.' He lowered his voice further. 'She didn't want me, you see, to have anything to do with you. You do see that? She threw things at me... once, anyway. A soup bowl, part of a bloody set, what's more. My oh my, Elsie! What a to-do!'

They had reached the door. He was still holding onto her. He had given her a nudge and she had begun to giggle. He looked down at her. He was still whispering because the woman couldn't have been far away and the other door was open.

'Not a day has passed when I haven't wondered, well, how are my little ones...? That's since. At the time, of course, the whole blessed shooting match on top of... You'd better run along.'

He pulled his arm free and pushed her forward into the corridor.

The other door was ajar. He was still whispering. 'Thank you for coming, Elsie. I'm actually just bloody sorry, that's all. Life, bloody life, that's what I say.' He glanced over his shoulder. 'It will not come again, will it?' They had reached the front door and he opened it. 'Look after yourself, Elsie, my daughter.'

On the way back to the seafront, those were the

two words she remembered. The wind was still blowing across the sea, making it sparkle and flash in the sun. The gulls still screeched above the harbour. All was as it had been, but the boats along the horizon had gone. She should never have told that man on the bus she'd sometimes wanted to kill her father. She should never have said that, his life not having turned out as he hoped it would.

VIII

'LIFE GOES ON,' Stan thought. He kept to himself, except for the little thieving jobs he did, that plus the warehouse. There was the telly. He was kept occupied. He didn't have to do much of the socialising at the warehouse. Sit about with a cup of tea. It was football mostly. All Arsenal supporters, bar one. He said he was Man City. Which he was, not a lot but enough to keep his end up. No one else gave a toss about Man City. Now it was the World Cup. He'd come south with his partner as was, but it hadn't worked out, that's what he told them. He'd be going back up north one day. They liked him well enough, always easy about days off, extra hours, filling in. Just heaving about these big bloody crates of furniture. There was Sherrill. It could go on for ever.

If he could get Johnny Boyd out of his mind. He'd phoned a bloke in Badger's 'entourage' (that was the sort of word Badger liked using) who'd given him a message from Badger, telling him to lie low. Ginger 'going the way of all flesh' had bust them up but memories were long, and he should keep an eye out. Badger had put all that behind him, once and for all. He preferred on the whole not to be inconvenienced. Oh yes, he'd heard that Johnny Boyd had been round to see his mother. When Stan phoned her she didn't mention that, she wouldn't want to worry him at the start of his new life.

He didn't phone so often now. He wanted to be on his own, just keep looking over his shoulder. He didn't talk to strangers. There'd been that freak-show woman on the bus, half barking about killing her mother and father. The only sort of person you were safe with, complete bloody misfits. After all those cons not giving a toss about what they'd done to anyone. And leading him to that nice little thieving job. He'd kept the photo from the silver frame for a week or so. Funny how a couple like that – dashing, the man was anyway – could have such an evil-looking daughter, with those thoughts in her head. The father looked like he fancied himself as a ladies' man, and his wife like one of the women he didn't fancy. Well, having to put up with a daughter like that, poor sods.

He was glad he'd never had kids. What would he tell them? Badger might not have told him to do it if he'd had kids. That was the thing. There might be more experienced men for the job, but they had families.

Badger had said that too. He remembered the bark of Badger's last words when he opened the door: 'Stanley!' He had his hands on the lapels of his jacket and his chest was puffed out. The friendliness had gone. It might have been hatred in his eyes. 'This meeting never occurred, did it? Get it right and the question never arises. If events occur to the contrary, I would prefer any acquaintance there might have been between us never to be mentioned. We all have our loved ones, don't we, Stanley?' Then he brushed him away with a flick of his hand.

There'd been a few more thieving jobs. Out in the suburbs. Detached houses where people went away for weekends. Anyone with half an eye could figure the phoney burglar alarms. If you were wrong, you scarpered. Frank never took risks. He'd never been to Frank's house. He didn't even know where he lived. They met in the same pub every Tuesday to plan the following week. He wouldn't do it if it wasn't for Sherrill and he didn't have to send a bit to his mother – not to disappoint the expectations of his womenfolk, as Badger might put it. It wasn't a bad life. Better than stuck away with all those cons day after day after day. Not that bad and good came into it any longer. It was a worse life for the woman on the bus. With nothing to live for except a mother and father she wanted to see the last of. What sort of a life was that?

Yesterday one of the men at the warehouse said he thought he recognised him. He'd lived in Manchester once. He'd shrugged as if to say, 'Who knows? Who cares?' At the time there hadn't been too much in the papers. Badger had told him to plead guilty: 'No fuss and botheration and superfluous proceedings.' He hadn't grown his moustache until he came out, and now he'd begun his beard. Well, he looked different even if he didn't feel it. The man at the warehouse seemed to have forgotten about it but just in case, he had a disagreement with the foreman and left. Frank told him about another warehouse on the same bus route. He always half expected to see that woman again. She'd stand out a mile. There'd be no more sitting next to her again. Why the fuck had he told her he'd killed someone? He might have said that if he hadn't. To take that look of stupid curiosity off her face. If that was what it was. To see how she'd look if she was frightened. But she hadn't looked any different at all.

IX

THE BICYCLES arrived on the morning of the twins'
sixth birthday. How could Elsie have known, Geoffrey
wondered, that they were ready for the next size up?
Not until Christmas, they'd decided. They shone, one
blue and one silver. The twins were spellbound, and in
their chattering excitement insisted they were taken at
once to the park to try them out. There was no gain-
saying them and that is what they did. Geoffrey and
Susan watched their joy and could not speak until the
twins were in bed.

'How did she know?' Geoffrey asked.

'Know what?'

'That they were ready for new bicycles?'

'Perhaps mother told her.'

Geoffrey phoned Dorothy, who said she couldn't
remember telling Elsie about the twins' bicycles. A
long time ago, perhaps, she'd mentioned they no

longer needed stabilisers. Geoffrey could not tell her that Elsie's generosity embarrassed them, that the twins believed even more now that their Aunt Elsie was a mysterious Fairy Godmother, not quite of this world, for they had never been allowed to see her. That night they knelt by their beds and prayed not for God's blessing on her, but to Elsie herself. Geoffrey could not say to his mother more than that it had been very kind and generous of her, and of course the twins would write their thank-you letters. Dorothy had nothing to say in reply. When Elsie next came she would simply say how much the twins had enjoyed their bicycles. She would not give Elsie a cheque then, so that it might appear she was paying for them. Giving the twins presents must be the biggest pleasure in her life. She said that to Geoffrey who knew that might well be so, but it was still an embarrassment. That was what Susan felt. If they had known that Elsie sometimes came up to spy on them, they might have hated her for that. They hated not knowing what to say to the twins. They considered saying she lived in Australia.

How had Elsie known? She'd known, because from time to time she'd travelled up by train, just to set eyes on them, her nephew and niece, to see how they were getting on. 'I love them,' she sometimes told herself out loud. She watched them growing up and changing, and they were beautiful to her. Often, very often, she summoned them before she slept, or dreamt of them playing in the National Trust gardens. It was almost as if she saw them, because she knew what they looked like, how they moved. There was a bench opposite their house where she could watch them unobserved, hidden behind a newspaper. As she came and left, she knew how to avert her face. She sometimes wore large dark glasses. It was better when it was raining because then she could hide herself with an umbrella. She never stayed long, only long enough to see them, to remind herself of them, so that her dreaming of them was up to date. She only cared that she knew how to bring them happiness. They were the only people in the world for whom she could feel no resentment, not even for a second. She would watch them grow up and leave home. She would try to go on seeing them when they went to university. There would be another generation of children for her to buy presents for, to see the looks on their faces. And one day in the far distant future they would know what she looked like; but perhaps they wouldn't, for there was no photograph of her, so far as she knew.

Geoffrey and Susan made sure that very special thank-you letters were written, with coloured photos of the twins riding their bicycles. 'If it gives her pleasure,' Susan asked, 'who are we...?' She had seen Elsie once when she'd first met Dorothy, who had decided, with Geoffrey's agreement, that his sister should be there. They had married in a registry office. Elsie had stayed away because she thought Geoffrey and Susan would want her to, so as not to attract attention.

Geoffrey had told her that of course they expected her to be there. She was his sister. Dorothy said the same. But Elsie didn't want to be the smallest part of what the guests would remember later. Susan said nothing, but could not hide her fearfulness when the matter was discussed that Elsie would have to appear in the wedding photographs. If she stood aside, people would remark on it and that would be something else to remember. When Susan said she was sorry Elsie could not have been there, Geoffrey knew she was lying.

Uncle Henry had looked around and asked Dorothy, 'Where is Elsie?' To which Pru had added, 'Yes, where is Elsie, for God's sake? Kept her well out of the way, have you, Dorothy?' 'It was her decision,' Dorothy had replied. 'She's not good on these occasions.' 'No wonder,' Pru had replied. She was sorry that Elsie wasn't there, Henry thought. If she had been she'd have made a point of not talking to anybody else and sod the bloody lot of them.

Elsie went up to see how happy the twins were with their new bicycles. It was wonderful the way they pedalled off down the street, and the way Geoffrey or Susan tried to keep up with them, telling them to be careful. What could be better than seeing two young children pedalling off into the distance on brand new bicycles? It really made life worth living.

X

STAN'S ROOM in Finsbury Park was on the top floor of a house with two other occupants. They were two elderly women with blonde hair who shouted at each other about the bathroom and kitchen they shared. He'd had a look at them once when the women were out. No wonder they rowed. The kitchen was filthy: the dishes were piled high in the sink, the gas stove was covered in grime, the black lino on the floor was torn, the unlit fridge door was open and the tins and milk and bread in it might have been there for ages. It had a rancid stink about it. The bathroom taps dripped and the bath was rusty and half full of water. Tubes and bottles lay about and the only towel which lay across the basin might have been a dishrag. With all that hatred they had for each other they hardly noticed him at all. Two stupid women quarrelling on and on and all the filth of it felt sometimes as if that was what the rest of his life would have to be like.

It was the opposite of how he'd been brought up. His mother was a meticulous kind of woman. She wanted everything in their little house in Manchester to be just so. They had to have their pride, what else had they got? was one of her sayings. He had to clean up after himself and tidy his bedroom. 'Keeping up standards' he could 'make something of himself'. In all the good trades, she told him, neatness and order were essentials, keeping everything shipshape. She fussed over his homework and made him write things again if there were too many crossings-out. He'd have to keep records for the Revenue and send invoices out and the like. She was proud of him when he began training as a gas-fitter. She didn't know he'd got caught up in the Badger mob, running the odd errand to make the extra bob or two. Mainly for her, it was. He never touched the stuff himself, seeing what it did to people. She was proud of him for his politeness, the way he was turned out with polish on his shoes and a crease in his trousers.

He kept his room very tidy, touching up the paint-work all the time, taking his sheets to the launderette every week, cleaning the sink and bath with Vim, fol-lowing her advice in his mind. It was a nice room and the noise from the street outside wasn't too bad after the rush hour was over. The window at the back looked out over the yards of other houses which were full of junk. If he leant out there was a gap where he could see the spire of a church and a couple of nice tall trees. There was a garden of sorts at the house at the end. It even had a lawn that needed mowing and what might be some sort of fruit tree. He felt secure there, a long way from where it happened, where they would never find him. From there to the shops round the corner, onto a bus to go to work and back again. He could tell her he'd settled down and could put the past behind him. He could tell her all about his room, every detail of it, and watch her smile that she'd taught him what she called his 'rudiments of life'.

He didn't often look out of the front window on to the street – just cars stopping and starting at the traffic lights and people walking along with shopping in plastic bags. But that evening, a man stopped and looked up at his window. Then he walked on and came back and looked up at his window again. The years had passed and he couldn't be sure. There was white now in the ginger hair, which had been cut short. But he was sure enough: it was Johnny Boyd, who'd drawn a finger across his throat when he was sent down. And then that note before he left the nick, saying his days were numbered.

He phoned one of his old mates who'd been close to Badger. He said he thought he'd seen Johnny Boyd, what was the talk?

His mate said he'd get back to him. The next evening he phoned to say that Badger had 'assimilated Ginger's associates a long time ago'. He couldn't speak for Ginger's brother, who was lucky not to have met his Maker at the same time as Ginger. 'One of life's inadequates', Badger had called him. Best lie low for a while was Badger's advice, not to make himself 'overly conspicuous' if he could help it. Stan thanked him. How was Badger? he asked. Badger was good, was the reply. Wished Stan well for old times' sake but, to be honest, his friend said, he wasn't too keen to be 'encumbered with bygones'.

He didn't see Johnny again for a week. He was getting on his bus when he saw him coming out of a café on the other side of the street, looking at his watch. It was that evening he saw Elsie again at the back of the bus on her way back from visiting her mother. She turned aside to look out of the window so that he wouldn't feel obliged to acknowledge her. When she looked back he raised a hand to her. After his stop had passed a seat became vacant next to her and he went and sat beside her. For a while they had nothing to say to each other, not even a greeting.

'How are you keeping?' he asked eventually.

'I'm very well, thank you,' she said. 'And yourself?'

'Not so bad.'

She let him see her face now. He did not flinch, looking hard into her eyes. Only her mother ever did that, trying to discern something, what she was thinking. But her eyes were too deep in her head and overshadowed by her brow. She could hardly see them in a mirror in broad daylight. She was glad she soon had to get off because the conversation had nowhere to go. It never did really, even with the other cleaners, who wouldn't want to pry into what sort of life she could live she would want to talk about. Stan had stayed on long after his own stop.

'I'm nearly home now. Two stops,' she said.

'I'm getting off there too,' he said.

They walked a little way together. This was her territory, where hands were sometimes raised at her with barely a glance, but they were raised, and she heard her name. It was the least they could do. She raised a hand back, but there could be no smile on either side. They could not know if she would rather not be greeted at all, to be left to herself. With Stan there they gave her a second glance. They were not chatting, just walking side by side, she slightly behind him and looking up a little, as though she was trying to sell him something.

They passed the Cypriot café where she sometimes went, with its grocery store next door. There, she could have been anyone. She chose, they took her money and gave her change, looking at her as quickly as they would at any other customer.

'Cup of coffee?' he said as they passed the café.

He was already leading her towards the door. There was nobody else there. They sat by the window and looked out of it until the owner came. They ordered coffee.

'Give us one of those buns too,' Stan said, looking at Elsie who nodded. 'Two buns then.' The owner went away, looking back over his shoulder as if he might have left something behind.

'You live near here?'

She pointed out of the window and said, yes, she did.

Stan didn't know how to go on, he didn't know how to ask. He had once said a shocking thing to her which she hadn't seemed to mind at all, that he had killed a man. He wished she would look at him, to see something in his face, his eyes, that told her she could trust him. It was the face he'd learnt from his mother as a child, clear and straight. She'd told him that when he went for a job, they always looked for trustworthiness, that was the thing. Badger used to say the same about dealing drugs: 'Your integrity is paramount', he used to say. That was the problem with Ginger, going behind Badger's back, you couldn't credit a word he said. 'No integrity in that neck of the woods,' was Badger's judgement.

'I don't even know your name,' he said.

'My name is Elsie.'

He offered his hand. 'Stan.'

He heard his mother's voice, whispering to him to be trustworthy. He saw Elsie's mother coming down her front path, crunching the gravel. A stern woman she'd looked, who wouldn't always be understanding. She wasn't someone to whom Elsie would take her doubts and worries. There was the look about her of not wanting to be bothered, especially not by Elsie, who'd already bothered her enough over the years.

'How's your mother then?' he asked as the coffee and buns were brought.

She made space for them on the table. 'She's very well, thank you.' She looked at him and there was an expression on his face of wanting to hear more – if she still felt like murdering her sometimes. 'I love my mother, if you must know. It was only a joke, what I said. I don't even see my father any longer.'

He relaxed and poured milk into his coffee, pushing the plate with the buns on it towards her. 'We say these things, don't we?'

'We shouldn't.'

There was a long pause. 'You don't know me from Adam,' he said. 'It's like this. There are certain paramount considerations.' That was Badger talking. He didn't want to hide behind Badger any more. His mother had always told him to be himself. 'The man I did time for was no good. He'd done one killing to everyone's certain knowledge and another bloke, both arms broken and a smashed skull. If you believed in capital punishment, well, it was your natural justice, wasn't it...?'

It was Badger talking again. It wasn't what he himself thought. He'd done it out of terror. He was staring into his coffee. Her hands were still and he could feel her looking at him, waiting.

'He's got this brother, you can imagine... I came down here... I've seen him.'

Elsie was still waiting, but not wanting to interrupt before he'd finished. She didn't want to be rude to him or make him feel uncomfortable with her. She had never seen fear on anyone's face before. Except Mr Wakefield worrying about his end before he had done right by his daughter. That was a different fear, not for something that waited just round the corner, but for what was coming closer at the end of a long flat road where thick shadows lay. She could not imagine being afraid of death, the little there was for her in life – except more and more lovely gardens of course, and an occasional glimpse of the sea. Seeing a garden in summer, though, she did often promise herself to come back and see it in the spring. Or in the autumn for that matter. She had nothing to say. There was nothing in her thoughts to share with him. She waited.

He pulled towards him the plate with the buns on it, then glanced up at her, inviting her to take one. She was staring at him, but there was nothing to tell from her deep-set eyes.

'Thing is, Elsie, he's found out where I live. Could you give me a bed for a day or two? Somewhere to kip down. It is possibly a request too far.' Badger again.

'Of course I will,' she said. 'Of course. But I do not want you to be under the impression that I am in favour of capital punishment. That would mean you not being here either.'

She wanted to touch his hand, which was fidgeting with the plate, trembling a little. But she did not know how to do that. Except with old Mr Wakefield, as he dropped off to sleep with all those drugs he was given. The others too, getting drowsy, wanting someone to talk to. She didn't want to be there when they woke up, to give them a fright, looking like one of those gargoyles who'd be a reception committee in hell, not a beautiful angel saying, 'Welcome, dear, to the afterlife...'

Stan looked at her a little longer. It might almost be a smile on her face. Or she was remembering things. 'You've nothing to fear from me, Elsie.'

'I know, Stan,' she replied, going up to the counter to pay for the coffee and buns which they hadn't touched. The owner glanced over her shoulder to see that.

'They're lovely buns,' she said. 'Very sticky. With lots of raisins. But we've lost our appetites.'

They walked off. She waddled ahead to show him the way, but also in case he didn't want to be seen with her. Her room was on the top floor but there was no one to see them as he followed her up the stairs. Stan smiled when he saw the room. It was just what his mother would have approved of, everything neat and tidy, even the tablecloth had been ironed and the green carpet dotted with flowers was new, or freshly cleaned. It was a nice bright room that did Elsie proud, his mother would say. She opened the door on a very small bathroom with a shower.

'It's not much,' she said. 'I'm sorry if the sofa isn't long enough but you could lay out the cushions on the floor if that is your preference.'

She opened the fridge, which also looked brand new; and the food inside was tidily arranged. She pulled back the curtains to show him the view of the houses and gardens opposite. 'Look,' she said, pointing at a garden four houses away. 'That's a magnolia. It's so lovely in spring.'

He couldn't believe his luck. She must have been able to tell how grateful he was without his having to say anything. She was standing there waiting for him to speak.

'Terrific,' he said. 'Really terrific. Thanks.'

She pointed at the other door. 'That's my bedroom. It's like another sitting room with a little telly which my mother bought me. I needn't disturb you but if you like we could have supper together.'

'I'll get a few things,' he said. 'Be back in a couple of hours. Get us some pizzas. How would that be?'

'I love pizza,' she said.

His room had been torn apart: everything, the curtains ripped, his clothes slashed, all the drawers were emptied onto the floor, every ornament shattered. The mirror was smashed in the bathroom, tins of food had been emptied onto the carpet. 'Hope to find you in next time' was scrawled with a red felt pen on the window.

He put his bathroom things into a shopping bag with one or two items of clothing and went back down the stairs. The two women were arguing loudly about the broken fridge, almost coming to blows.

'You can help yourself to mine,' Stan said. 'I'm not coming back.'

'He was asking after you. Such a nice polite man he was.'

'Ever so nice,' the other one said, then raised her voice. 'Stinks. That's what it does. Fucking stinks!"

He told Elsie what had been done to his room, trying to make it sound not too out of the ordinary, so as not to alarm her.

She tried to match the casualness in his voice. 'So meeting me might have been quite timely?' she said.

'You could have saved my life, Elsie,' he said.

He wanted to bring an expression of pleasure to that warped face. She moved her hand a small way towards his across the table.

'I'm always glad to be of assistance,' she said.

In fact, she was very glad indeed. As glad as she had ever been. Even more glad than the day she'd taken Mr Wakefield's letter to the bank and seen that contented smile on his face she had never seen there before.

'This is a lovely pizza,' she said.

Stan went to see Sherrill the following evening. The little girl was sick and wouldn't stop crying. She told him, 'Not tonight, Stan.' He gave her a hundred quid and told her he might not be able to come round for quite a long time. She said the girl's father had been round that afternoon, 'expecting his dues and not a penny of support'. He couldn't tell if she'd been crying or it was just that the child had exhausted her. He held her tight, which reminded him of everything. Tears came to his eyes, that he'd no longer be there for her. She'd often told him he treated her like a princess, spoiling her rotten, and now he was leaving her alone with that shithouse. If things had been different, he'd have liked to have taken her off somewhere, started all over again. But things weren't different. She didn't even know what he'd done. Love was useless sometimes. He'd get money to her somehow from time to time... He said it then: 'I love you' and she gave him a squeeze, not saying it back. Life was just going on somehow. The child had at last fallen asleep. 'I'm too tired, Stan. Take care of yourself.' She wanted him to go. She wanted to rest, to sleep. She wouldn't have been like that towards him if she'd known what he'd done. There could never be a lasting love for him with that secret to be kept, waiting to come out at any time.

When he returned to Elsie's room he phoned his mother. He told her he'd decided to move on, so she couldn't phone him at his old address. She used to tell him she liked to have a picture of it in her mind. So he'd sent her a sketch of it and three photographs taken from different angles. She liked to think of him being comfortable in tidy surroundings after all that had happened. He told her he would pack everything very carefully.

'I'm glad you're all right,' she said at the beginning. 'I was worried about you.'

'Why, Mum? There's nothing to worry about.'

Then she told him. 'This man came round. Very fat and sweaty with ginger hair. Asked me if I knew where you were. Said I didn't have the faintest. You'd disappeared into thin air.'

'Was that all?'

'He gave me a phone number and said if I ever heard about you, give him a bell. I asked him what he wanted to know for anyway. He said it was just a bit of business... Are you there, Stanley?

'I'm here, Mum.'

'It's to do with what happened, isn't it?'

'Could be.'

'You just bugger off into nowhere, Stanley. Find somewhere nice. Make a nice little home for yourself.'

He'd never heard her use a word like that before.

'I'll phone, Mum. You're not to worry.'

'Of course I worry, you daft thing.'

He phoned his friend again to find out if there was anything new. He said that Badger was 'a trifle indisposed at the present moment in time', he'd phone back. When he did, it was to say that Ginger's brother was drinking himself silly and was of no interest to Badger any longer. 'He's a spent force, you could call it. But still saying he'll get you. Better to be honest about it for old times' sake.' Badger had put it about that Stan had acted off his own initiative. No one knew that Badger had told him he didn't want any harm to come to him or his loved ones, 'that lovely mother of yours'. His friend said Badger wouldn't expect to hear from him again. Those weren't his words. 'He thinks the time has arrived to draw a discreet line…' Stan didn't let him finish, said a polite thank you and hung up.

He decided to tell Elsie everything. It wasn't like confiding in anyone else. He didn't want her to be afraid of him. Though it was impossible to tell from her face, her hand moved a little way towards him over the table and sometimes she nodded. He wanted her to say she understood, but she only seemed to be taking it all in.

Once he was tired of talking and said, almost angrily, 'You must think I'm pretty much scum and you'd be well rid of me.' She didn't shake her head or nod. 'You've only got to say the word.'

Her hand rested on the table not far from his and she withdrew it slightly. She cleared her throat. 'How can you say that, Stan? I am not a judge. The world is the way it is.'

He stood up and turned on the television and she began cooking them pasta for their supper.

He told her he'd have to be out most evenings that week. Frank had found a few jobs out in the suburbs.

Nothing big. He'd only be driving the van. Last Tuesday Frank had said he was thinking of packing it all in. He didn't have the stamina for it any longer and he didn't want to be inside any more at his age, he had his obligations. Stan had never told Elsie about Frank and the jobs they'd done. She would have asked him not to do that any longer. And he wouldn't have done. He owed her that. Especially after pinching that silver frame with the photograph of her mum and dad on their wedding day. She had told him so little about herself. She'd said there was nothing really to tell: her father going off with another woman and now being old; a brother who had twins; and her mother whom she saw from time to time and with whom she got on quite well, there were no hard feelings. There were no hard feelings about her father either, not any longer.

Two weeks passed. When Stan was in, they ate supper and watched television together. He told her more about himself, especially about his mother, how neat and tidy she was, bringing him up to have standards. 'She'd approve of the way you've done your flat, that's for sure,' he told her. At weekends Elsie went to visit gardens. He didn't want to go with her. He said he wasn't a gardens sort of bloke. It was the thought of being seen by people hidden behind trees a long way off, keeping him in view. Being seen with her would draw attention, people wondering what had brought them together. He felt more and more he was being followed, that Johnny Boyd was getting closer. After he'd got his cards from the warehouse, he thought he got a clear glimpse of him when he was about to catch the bus back to Elsie's place. So he took the tube, changing several times before he was sure he had shaken him off.

He had to tell Elsie. It was the risk he was putting her in, he said. Saying it, he knew it was true, that he didn't care much about his own life any longer. It couldn't go on like this. He said he would have to move on. He wanted to get a long way away. Start a new life. But it would still be the same old life, empty and useless. He said he appreciated what she'd done for him. 'You're a good soul, do you know that Elsie?' She nodded and said it was nothing. He didn't even know if his gratitude meant anything to her.

'Glad I could be of assistance,' she said. She wanted him to know she had been well brought up too.

He stood up, wanting to put an arm round her shoulder, but she might not have wanted that. She seemed to draw away from him. He was standing half behind her and it was she who took the initiative, resting her fingers on the back of his hand for an instant, unless it was an accident as she stood up to clear away the plates and pour Stan another beer.

XI

DOROTHY WAITED for Elsie's monthly visit. As always, she wondered what they would find to talk about. Their lives had that sameness about them. Elsie had found another cleaning job in a nursing home and there was little she could be expected to say about mopping floors and cleaning toilets etc. 'I do take pride, Mother,' Elsie had told her once. That was something she'd always known about Elsie, as soon as she knew she was not like other people. She took great care over her homework. But in between she often sat there dreaming, her head in her hand. 'A penny,' she'd asked her more than once. What dreams she had Dorothy could not imagine, except of being other than she was. She heard the crunch of the gravel on the drive. Poor Elsie. What more could she do? Increase her allowance? That would be something. So that she could travel wherever the fancy took her, to see her gardens, to live whatever dreams they gave her.

Elsie sipped her tea too hurriedly. Why did her mother always look as if she had just had her hair done? It seemed to hold her face stiff like an uncomfortable, tight helmet which might fall off if she moved her head too suddenly. It looked too as if she had spent a long time doing her make-up, putting on too much at first, then having to take some of it off. Was it only for her that she took that much trouble? Once, her mother had never looked at her for very long. Now it was different. Now, it was as if she was trying not to stare but at the same time was forcing herself not to look away, trying not to seem sad, or not glad enough to see her. Her eyes expressed nothing. Then, suddenly, they were filled with apology, even grief. What was it her father had seen, or not seen in her? Elsie felt she was looking down on them, hovering, ready to fly away to where the trees were. Her mother was talking.

'Your Uncle Henry is going to live in Spain. Of course, I told you that. He's there now, finalizing things.'

'I expect it's very nice with all that sunshine,' Elsie said. 'Will he invite you there?'

'I expect so, but I won't go.'

Elsie would not ask why. It was not the sort of question she asked her mother. It was odd that she showed so little curiosity about visiting Spain. What other news was there? Dorothy sighed, looking out of the window as if at some eyesore that ought to have been removed a long time ago. 'He's taken the cottage off the market for the time being. His cottage, I need hardly remind you.' Elsie only nodded. 'He did say Geoffrey could use it, or I could for that matter.' She nodded at her father's desk. 'Left me the keys. Told me if I was so minded, could I nip down and check it was all right? Fat chance of that.'

Elsie did not need to ask. She was close to the desk and could reach out for the keys. She held them in her hand as if weighing them.

'Do you think I could...?'

'Well, of course, Elsie.' For a moment she wasn't so sure. 'Well, if... I don't see why not, but...'

Elsie held onto the keys. 'What about Geoffrey?' she asked.

'It's much too far for him. He wouldn't dream of it, to be frank, not after what Uncle Henry said to him last time.' She imitated his voice. 'We need rather more notice than that, old chap.'

Elsie held tighter to the keys as if Dorothy wanted her to put them back on the table, to remove all thought of her going to stay in the cottage, perhaps taking some of her friends there from the hospital or wherever she worked now.

'Elsie, dear, I thought I'd add a bit to your allowance.' She held out her hand for the keys, but Elsie thought she wanted another cup of tea. 'These trips you make and train fares being what they are.'

Elsie said nothing about the increase in her

allowance. She'd always been impeccable about her pleases and thank-yous. That was what she had been taught, as if perfect manners would make up a little for the impression she gave otherwise. She had only been there for half an hour. The keys were still held tight in her hand.

'I think I'd like to go down there for a time, Mother, if Uncle Henry doesn't mind. I can give it a thorough cleaning, touch up the paintwork and things like that.'

'Oh I don't think…' Dorothy began. She had no idea that Elsie had ever done any painting.

'I did my kitchen and bathroom, Mother. Gloss and emulsion. Non-drip. I told you.'

'I didn't remember…'

Then she recalled Henry's letter, saw his face as he put a price on the Spode china and the cottage. A sort of glossy, knowing-best face, saying, 'You've got a bargain there, Dotty.' One of the last things their father had said to her: 'Better watch Henry. Getting a bit vulgar, if you ask me. Don't stand for any nonsense.' Henry was always putting her in her place, passing his exams with flying colours etc. and she good at nothing much. She saw Henry's face at her wedding, looking across at Robert, as if he was thinking, 'Well, no surprise there that she couldn't do better than that.' She'd overheard him say to Pru, 'Common little bugger.'

When Robert left her Henry had said, 'Good

riddance if you ask me.' It wasn't good riddance to her. It was heartbreaking.

'Of course, Elsie, you must stay there as long as you like. Of course you must. Keep an eye on it for me. I know Uncle Henry will be very grateful...'

Elsie opened her handbag and dangled the keys above it. 'Can I take the keys now?'

There was nothing to tell from her face as usual, but there was an eagerness, a softness in that croaky voice Dorothy hadn't heard before and she thought, 'When has Elsie ever had anything to look forward to?' She would get by, she would cope, she wouldn't allow life to get her down. When talking about the National Trust gardens, she spoke as if she was reading from a brochure.

'By all means, Elsie. By all means.'

Elsie dropped the keys into her handbag and went to kiss her mother. She had always wanted to spare her the unhappiness of worrying about her as she went about her business in the world. She'd often said during their meetings, 'You're not to worry. I'm really fine. I've got my nice flat, thanks to you, my job.' Things like that. She couldn't make her voice sound as if she really meant it and wasn't just trying to cheer her mother up. But she didn't know if she did mean it, if she was fine at all. When her mother asked her if she was happy, she was never sure what happiness was. Or unhappiness. From almost the very beginning she'd had nothing to compare them with. Now, it might be becoming different. If she could take Stan down to the cottage to make another fresh start.

'Don't worry, Mother,' she said. 'You're really not to worry. I've been a cleaner nearly all my life and it's too late in the day to change the habits of a lifetime.'

XII

STAN WASN'T SURE at first, going that far, all the way to
Dorset. He didn't know anything about the countryside, couldn't imagine living there. It would be further
away from his mother. It would be hard to get used to
Elsie always there, though he could find no fault in
her. She would do what had to be done, and keep
everything clean. He wondered if there would be a
garden. Still, it would be safe. If he could hole up
there, take stock. He could let his hair and beard grow
longer. He stood by her window, looking down at the
street, and thought that any day now he'd see that
ginger head again. He went to the window at the back
and looked at the trees she'd pointed out with that
excitement in her voice. Just a tree. The following
evening he said to Elsie while she did the washing-up.
'I'll get a car, Elsie.'

She turned. As usual, there was no smile, or any

other expression, to be seen, but she wiped her hands on her apron and gave him the thumbs-up sign.

The cottage was set apart at the end of the village. A 'for sale' sign was lying by the gate. Stan carried their suitcases down the front path. Elsie noticed that it had been freshly paved, but weeds and grass were growing through some of the cracks. The grass needed mowing and there were weeds around the shrubs in the flowerbeds. She wondered if Stan would give her a hand tidying it as his mother might want him to. She had such a kindly face in the photo Stan had shown her, but she wasn't smiling. Kindly, but sure of herself and what was right.

They wandered around the cottage without speaking, Elsie running her finger through the thin layers of dust. The furniture and carpets and curtains looked quite new and the beds in the two bedrooms upstairs had patchwork quilts on them. The kitchen was fully equipped and there were a hoover and cleaning materials in the cupboard under the stairs. Elsie glanced at Stan, wondering what he was thinking. 'Very nice, Elsie. Very nice,' he said from time to time. It would give him something to do while he waited, she did not know what for. Perhaps he could invite his mother down to see it. She opened the windows to let in the fresh air. The garden at the back had an apple tree in it with little apples forming after the fall of the blossom. The grass was even longer than the lawn at the front. There was probably a lawnmower in the shed at the bottom of the garden, with tools lined up. It was the way Uncle Henry would want to do things, everything spick and span and in its place. There was even a new-looking television set. She wouldn't let him down, or Aunt Pru, who was bossy but had once been kind to her a very long time ago, taking her hand even and running on ahead in the park.

There were two bedrooms and Elsie asked which one he'd prefer. He said the decision was hers, so she chose the one overlooking the garden. He was glad about that because he wanted to keep an eye on the road. She offered to make up his bed but he said very definitely that he'd do that, but thanks all the same. He wasn't going to have her skivvying for him. He nearly added that he'd tidy his room himself too, but she might think that was her job, something she was good at, and he didn't want to hurt her feelings.

'I'll go and get us some provisions in,' Stan said, having opened all the kitchen cupboards to see what tins there were, and making a list. He showed it to Elsie and she told him he'd thought of everything. They'd seen a village store but he said he'd go to the Budgen's in the last town they'd driven through. While he was away, she'd at once begin wiping away the dust and then hoover. She wanted it to be spotless for him when he came back. She wanted it to be a peaceful place where he could consider calmly what to do next with his life, almost like a home. She opened her purse but he told her not to bother.

He drove off, trying to work out what he'd do in a place like that, nice and comfy though it was without a doubt, how he'd spend his days. The next day he'd have to get rid of the car in some back street somewhere and buy one of their own. He wished he knew what sort of money Elsie had, though there was still some of Badger's left. They had to have a car, there was no doubt about that, village shop or no village shop. They'd have to drive around and the sea wasn't far. He wasn't going to rush into anything. He'd tried to tell Elsie on the way down how grateful he was and now, having seen the cottage, he was even more so. He wondered how he could pay her back. Perhaps just having someone round to look after was sort of a reward. She'd pointed at the garden on the way in and said, 'We'll have to see to that, Stan, won't we?' He could do the garden, that was it, keep it neat and tidy. His mother would be amazed if she could see him living in a perfect little country cottage, complete with garden back and front. These were his thoughts as he bought the provisions and drove back and opened the door to find the cottage so clean, to see Elsie with a can of polish in her hand, bringing a shine to the table.

They sat at the table with cups of tea and digestive biscuits. Stan smiled at her and couldn't stop himself from nodding and saying more than once, 'This is the life, Elsie.' Each time she replied, 'It is, isn't it?' She was happy, telling him she'd turned on the hot water and switched on the electricity at the fuse box.

'Everything is in perfect working order,' she said.

'I'll be buying us a car tomorrow. Do you have any preferences as to make and suchlike?'

She was beginning to ask what was wrong with the car they'd driven down in but Stan interrupted her. 'Sorry, Elsie, there was a shortage of time, wasn't there? They'll have it back in one piece. Look at it that way.'

She nodded. 'I've always liked a black car,' she said. 'Nothing too racy.'

Stan bowed towards her. 'Your wish will be granted, my lady,' he said, thinking again he wished he had an idea of what contribution she had to make to things.

The days passed. Elsie phoned Dorothy to say that the cottage was fine and she was looking after it as Uncle Henry would wish. Even the garden. A man had come to say he'd been asked to tidy it up once a fortnight, looking back at the front gate as if it was a means of escape. If he wasn't needed, it was all the same to him, thank you, with all the other demands on his time. He was almost as short as Elsie, so he couldn't avoid looking at her. He began scratching his hair as if suddenly attacked by fleas. There were gaps in his teeth and his voice was hoarse as though he was getting it worked up for an argument. He caught a glimpse of Stan carrying a mug of coffee from the kitchen.

'Staying here long, will you be, then?' he asked.

'We're only caretaking it for my uncle...'

The man had another look at Stan and was not

going away. She glanced at Stan too. He was just standing there with the mug in his hand. With his beard growing and his thick, uncombed hair and frown, he had the expression of someone looking for a fight. She didn't want that impression of him spoken about in the village. Suddenly she remembered one of the ideas she'd had of her father, steering a ship through stormy seas. She'd imagined him like that when she'd seen the programmes on television about the lives of fishermen.

'My cousin has been at sea,' she said. 'For a long time. And is having a rest from it.'

That seemed to satisfy the man. 'A life on the ocean wave, is that it? Seeing the world,' he said. 'I'm all for it myself.' He raised a hand to Stan as from one seafaring man to another and went back down the path, looking left and right at the newly mown lawn, shaking his head.

'So that's what I am,' Stan said. 'Never been to sea in my life, except on that bloody ferry. Sick as a dog.'

He looked at her and laughed. She had never heard him laugh before. She could imagine how he would have been if nothing had happened to him; enjoying a joke with the lads, they called it. She wished she could laugh too, without it making her face look as if she was in pain.

'We'll have to keep it up,' he said, laughing again a little, 'at the village shop. Shiver my timbers, if that isn't a fine piece of haddock you've got there, hauled up from the deep.'

He had no idea if that was the sort of thing seamen said.

'No, Stan,' Elsie said. 'We'll have to think of better expressions than that.'

She'd never spoken to him like that before, like a reprimand, like that supervisor in Edgar Wakefield's hospital who'd found an unmopped area in the toilet which hadn't been her job, but she'd apologized as if it had been. It was somehow easier for her to get into trouble because in the end they felt sorry for her. If she couldn't help her face, they might wonder if she couldn't help anything else. She hadn't wanted the new girl to get into trouble, what with her mother having no husband and five children to look after.

'Ay, ay, Captain,' Stan said with a salute. 'I'd better get one of those hats.'

She phoned Dorothy twice a week. Uncle Henry was still in Spain. They were having trouble with the builders and lawyers and had to stay on the spot to sort things out. She hadn't told him that Elsie was looking after the cottage. He might have told her that Elsie couldn't stay there with friends pitching up from the cleaning fraternity and her being too nice and kind to turn them away. That was how he had put it once. Dorothy couldn't imagine Elsie all alone in a cottage in the country. There must be difficulties and worries, so she said she'd have some more money paid into her account from the deposit Uncle Henry had given her.

'What do you do with your time, Elsie?'

'There is a bus, Mother, to take me about, especially to the sea, of course.'

'I expect there are some nice people there. There is more friendliness in the country, so I've been told.'

That wasn't what Uncle Henry had told her: they didn't like outsiders much. Dorothy thought it was probably Uncle Henry they didn't like. She could imagine him lording it a bit, striding along the roads with a walking stick and wearing one of those tweed caps. She couldn't imagine Pru there at all. But she was a reader, like Elsie, and that might be enough for her, plus the drives to restaurants where she would talk in a loud voice.

'I haven't really met anyone yet, Mother. Except a man who came to do the garden, which we can manage ourselves. So we can save Uncle Henry money.

Dorothy hesitated. Elsie's speech was never very distinct, the vowels swallowed as if words got stuck in her throat, struggling to reach her tongue. 'We?' There was a pause. 'Are you having friends to stay, Elsie? I do understand. It must be very hard to turn them away.' She suddenly felt relieved that Elsie had any friends at all.

'Oh no, Mother. Please tell Uncle Henry that I won't have any friends to stay. Nobody knows where I am except you.'

In fact they had met two or three people in the village, apart from the gardener. When they went to the store, she was asked point-blank by the woman at the counter if she would be staying in the cottage long. She was a tall woman who had her hair tied back, which seemed to stretch her face and raise her eyebrows. She would have an inquisitive look whatever she said, looking down at their purchases as if she couldn't believe people could possibly want to buy things like that. 'Will that be all?' was made to sound as if it was far too much or hardly worth the bother.

Elsie said she was looking after the cottage for her uncle who was in Spain.

'Off the market, is it?'

Elsie didn't quite know the answer to this and said she would make enquiries. The woman was watching Stan carefully as he packed their purchases in a plastic bag. Stan had said nothing and the woman made it clear, her eyebrows even higher, that it was about time he did. As he finished filling the bag, he looked up and saw she was expecting him to say something. He picked out a tin of sardines.

'Miss the old briny,' he said in an extra gruff voice.

'I beg your pardon?' the woman asked, as if he'd said something critical of the store and the quality of the sardines she sold.

Elsie would have loved to have smiled then, but

the woman would only have taken it as a snarl. It was the funniest thing she had heard for a long time: Stan missing the briny. He was only managing to grunt now and had turned to go.

She stared at the woman, who looked away with a sigh, not quite of disgust, but as if to say, there'd been times when customers weren't like this, not like this at all.

Elsie remembered a song from long ago which she half sang: 'A life on the ocean wave…'

Stan turned and opened his eyes wide. 'Blimey!' he said. Then to the shopkeeper, 'We seafaring folk…'

Out in the street he gave her a nudge. 'Snooty cow!' he said.

There had been another woman in the shop, ahead of them, who had paid them no attention. Now, she hurried a few paces after them.

'I'm so sorry,' she said. 'You're at Rosetree Cottage… I saw you… I'm just beyond… I just thought if there's anything… I'm so sorry…'

It must have been having a closer look at them, Elsie thought, out in the open air. Stan was frowning as if trying to keep up with what the woman was saying, as if he hadn't understood it all and couldn't be bothered with trying to. The woman was flushed. There was a fixed smile on her face, as if being kept in readiness. Behind her glasses her eyes sparkled. Perhaps there were tears there, or it might have been embarrassment. A gust of wind blew her thin grey hair apart and she held her hand there. Elsie had to say something.

'It's lovely to meet you,' she said. She glanced at Stan and wished he'd take that suspicious look off his face. Here was someone from whom they need fear nothing. 'We should be glad to make your acquaintance further.'

The woman was too flustered to continue. Elsie knew her voice hadn't sounded friendly at all and Stan was still staring. Why didn't he say something too? 'Wouldn't we, Stanley?' Sailors were supposed to be all cheery and welcoming.

'Do come and see us,' the woman said. 'My granddaughter is...' But she stopped as if having too much to say. The smile was now apologetic, even ashamed. 'Do come,' she repeated and left them.

'Queer fish,' Stan said. 'We don't want too much to do with neighbours, do we? Wagging tongues and that?'

Elsie remembered one day when she was working in the garden, she had seen a girl skipping along the lane, who had watched her for a moment or two through a gap in the hedge. That was how it had been once long ago, watching the other girls, slim and skipping and carefree, and very beautiful. There were the songs they used to sing in the choir. At first everyone could join, but then there was some weeding out to do when the school entered a contest, and she was the first to go. She'd wished she didn't have to audition in front of the other doubtfuls. She was told she was nearly in tune but an octave too low. With her throat feeling so narrow she couldn't go any higher without squeaking. After the audition, they did ask her to be responsible for keeping the music in proper order. One other girl didn't get in the choir either. Her name was Deirdre and she didn't seem to be able to sing in tune at all. She ran from the room in tears. Elsie had told her they could look after the books together but she went on and on saying it wasn't her fault she couldn't sing.

When they skipped, she could hear their laughter a long way off. She wanted to dance with them too, round and round. It was a long time before she knew she never would. Once she practised it when no one was looking and tripped up over her own feet. But she had loved them so much, looking at their high spirits, and they'd even come to talk to her, so she hadn't minded there would be no place in that world for her. She could dream of it, holding their hands, going round and round.

That evening the woman came round with a bowl of raspberries.

'Lucy and I picked these this afternoon,' she said. 'I've got a little vegetable garden and thought...'

Beyond her, Elsie could see the child lingering at the gate, throwing a ball up and down. The woman looked back at her.

Elsie couldn't be sure that Stan would want her to

be invited in. He'd said often enough they must keep to themselves. 'That is so very kind of you,' she said. Her words often had to be exaggerated to express what she couldn't say with her voice. It would be lovely to sound appreciative with a lilt in her voice as other people could. 'Thank you so much.'

The woman handed over the bowl, again glancing back at the girl. Without the bowl to hold, her hands became fidgety.

'You see, she's staying with me and I don't know… There's nothing…'

Her face had become flushed and she stroked back her hair as though a wind had ruffled it. Elsie nodded. Perhaps she shouldn't care what Stan might think about inviting her in. She nodded, as if to say, Go on.

'I've lived here for ages but don't really know anyone. There aren't any other children of her age and I…' She searched for Elsie's eyes, wanting to know how to continue. 'You see her parents are not getting on frightfully well and my daughter, that's her mother, thought she could get away from it all with me… It's so lovely to have her… I don't mean…'

She saw Stan come out of the kitchen over Elsie's shoulder.

'Hallo, there!' he said in a cheery sort of mocking voice. Elsie was worried that he might say something like 'Shiver my timbers!'

The woman was now very flustered. 'I'm so

sorry. I haven't introduced myself. Isabel Waters.' She pointed back up the lane. 'The next cottage along.'

'Stormy Waters more my line of country,' Stan said. It was very silly, Elsie thought, but at least he was sounding more welcoming.

The girl was still at the gate, throwing the ball high and not always catching it.

'She's not all that shy really,' Mrs Waters said. 'Come along, darling, and meet the neighbours,' she called out.

But the girl took no notice.

Elsie saw the girls all dancing in a ring, hand in hand, the skipping. She heard the laughter of long ago. 'She would be welcome here at any time,' she said. 'There are some games.'

Mrs Waters suddenly turned and went back down the path. Her smile had hardly changed at all. The girl said something to her that Elsie could not hear. It had sounded quite cross.

She closed the door and Stan handed her a glass of Cinzano, which was her special treat at the beginning of the evening.

'What bloody games are those, I'd like to know?' he said.

In a cupboard she had discovered a number of board games that Uncle Henry and Aunt Pru had bought. Or perhaps left there by friends they'd lent the cottage to.

'There are lots of them,' she said.

'All right then, if you say so. Anyway...'

He couldn't tell Elsie he didn't want the girl hanging about. It was her cottage. He wanted to move on, soon. He'd bought an old Astra for two thousand pounds and drove quite far, trying to think up ideas. There were the building jobs. He could finish his NVQ training and go back to gas-fitting. He phoned his mother every week and she always asked when he was coming to see her. She said she missed his little visits. And Sherrill. She told him the child was better and she hadn't seen her father in ages and she missed him too. She reminded him over the phone of some of the things they'd done, sometimes giggling, sometimes sighing.

He'd thought Elsie would get on his nerves in no time, that correct way she had with talking, speaking being a bit of an effort, so she had to work at it. But they had become at ease in each other's company. If he felt cooped up in the evening he could just drive off to the movies, or a quiet pub. She never asked where he was going. They had begun to address each other in nautical terms: 'Ahoy there, Captain!' or 'Heave ho, my hearties!' when he was digging in the garden. Or 'What shall we do with the drunken sailor?' when she brought him his second lager. 'You keep it all very ship-shape,' he'd tell her, or admire the way she scrubbed the decks when she mopped the linoleum floor in the kitchen.

'You keep your cabin spotless,' she once told him.

'In my ocean-going days, can't say I recall sailors making up one another's bunks,' he replied.

She entered into the spirit of it. In fact, from dreaming about her father on the ocean wave she had more phrases than he did. When she sang, 'What shall we do with the drunken sailor?' in her deep voice, he staggered across the room with a loud, short laugh. She couldn't imagine being happier than this. But one day it would have to come to an end. Dorothy had told her that Uncle Henry was still settling in in Spain and the legal problems were 'quite horrendous'.

'Does he mind me being here?' Elsie asked.

'I think he might actually be quite pleased,' she lied. 'Have any of your friends…?'

'No, Mother, none of my friends.'

'What do you do with yourself all day long?'

'There is a bus, Mother. Two buses. One takes me to the sea. There are birds. It's lovely. Even doing nothing, a bit of shopping and gardening and touching up and…'

Dorothy became impatient with all this. 'So long as you're happy, dear,' she said.

When Stan phoned his mother to tell her he'd moved, she said she was feeling a little bit poorly and might have to go into hospital. So he gave her the telephone number and told her to pin it above her telephone in place of his London number to catch the eye in an emergency. She wasn't very good with paper, forgetting where she'd put it or, wanting to keep things looking tidy, just chucking it away. So he made her do that before he hung up. When he phoned a week later she said she was feeling a whole lot better and he must stop all that worrying about her. She said she must have thrown away his telephone number and could he tell her again what it was. Oh yes, she added, that man had come again, but he soon went away without hardly saying anything. Stan closed his eyes. If she was feeling better there was no need for that any longer, he said.

XIII

Lucy came the following afternoon. When Elsie opened the door she was standing there with another bowl of raspberries. She looked cross at first, as though it wasn't her idea. 'If you must know,' she whispered, as if sharing a secret, 'I picked these all by myself.'

For a moment Elsie could not reach out to take the bowl. Something had overcome her, something important which all her life she had been missing. She saw that Lucy had a slight squint and the sun was in her eyes. Her lips were apart and there was a metal band on her upper teeth. She looked hard at Elsie, at first with curiosity, then with disappointment, as if she wanted to know what Elsie was thinking, then had to give up. She pulled back the bowl.

'Oh well,' she said. 'Admittedly raspberries aren't to everyone's taste. I expect you've had a bellyful already.'

'Oh no, no!' said Elsie. 'Oh dear! We loved them, we absolutely loved them and gobbled them up last night, to the very last one. They were lovely!'

Especially now, she wished she could put some proper feeling into her voice. But Lucy did not seem to mind at all. The sun had gone in and her eyes were wide. They were almost golden, looking in two slightly different directions. It made her look cunning, so you could never be absolutely sure what she was thinking. Then she smiled, exposing the band to the full. It was like a smile when everything suddenly becomes all right after some long sorrow, or as if woken from a nightmare. She handed over the bowl, peering past Elsie into the cottage.

Elsie stood aside. 'You've got it looking really quite nice, I must say,' Lucy said.

'Would you like to come in?' Elsie asked.

Lucy moved past her and stood in the middle of the room, looking around. Elsie had been clearing out the cupboard with the games and they were lying on the table.

'Oh look!' said Lucy. 'Scrabble and snakes and ladders and mah jong and even chess. Do you play chess by any chance? It's probably the most ancient game there is, invented by the Chinese.'

Elsie had learnt the rules from one of the inmates in her first residential home, but as soon as they started playing, he seemed to forget them, except when she got something wrong. He had many other things to talk about in his long life, becoming increasingly fearful of how much he had forgotten. As he spoke he moved the pieces here and there, often not waiting his turn, as if it was a ridiculous thing to be doing when there was so much remembering to be done.

'A bit,' said Elsie. 'I mean I bet I'm not half so good as you.'

'I'm a bit of a rabbit too,' Lucy said, taking the box of pieces and setting them out on the board.

There was a table on the patio leading to the back garden. 'Let's sit there,' Elsie said.

Elsie did not want to pry. It was one of the worst things, such as when people wanted to be kind to her and show an interest, but were only curious to find out how awful her life must be. None of the questions was ever any good at all: like did she have any brothers and sisters, what sort of work she did, even where she was going on holiday. Then she was suddenly ignored. Nobody asked what it was like to be very ugly and suddenly to be asked a lot of questions. Her natural expression was of someone wanting to be left well alone. She was glad it wasn't that sort of friendly look some ugly people tried to have. But Lucy only wanted to talk.

'If you must know, my mother and father are not getting along, so granny said I could go and live with her until it all blows over.'

'Let's hope then…' Elsie began, moving her bishop so that her queen was exposed.

Lucy laughed. 'Look! That's even more useless than me. There's no prospect of that, unfortunately. They absolutely hate each other, completely hate each other. The shouting, shouting! I have to go to my room and block my ears.'

Elsie muttered she was sorry and tried another move. 'Is it...?' she began.

But she had no idea what questions could be asked. She glanced at Lucy's face, concentrating hard on the game. There should have been something very sad or hurt or desperate in her face, but her eyes had become suddenly old. She was biting her lower lip, as if the band had fastened her teeth there. It was something she suddenly understood; she had been there most of her life. It was beyond caring. It was knowing what it was to be without hope, it was deciding to get on with things. She wanted more than she had wanted anything to reach out and grip Lucy's hand.

Lucy stopped concentrating. 'Well, I'm not going there or you'll probably checkmate me or something.' She had heard Elsie's question.

'Actually, if you must know, my father found another woman or something and he thought she was playing around. I don't know. How do I know, for Pete's sake? They just hate each other. I want them to be together more than anything in the whole world, but fat chance of that, thank you very much.'

Elsie moved a knight to threaten Lucy's queen. She thought, 'Lucy has made it impossible ever to feel sorry for myself again.' She was thinking so hard about her mother and father that she might not have noticed her queen was being threatened. Elsie pointed at the knight. 'Look out!' she said.

'I'm not blind, you know,' Lucy said. She touched her queen but did not move it. 'When they shout, they always say "You only think about yourself. Can't you even think about Lucy? Selfish bitch. Selfish bastard." As if I'd gone to live in Australia or somewhere. When I cried it only made them argue about whose fault it was and whose job it was to make me feel better…'

She moved her queen to safety. 'At least now you have your granny,' Elsie said. 'Perhaps while they try to sort things out. I'm sure they love you.'

Lucy sighed. 'I don't actually care any more. I just want to be grown up and have people of my own. I don't know if they love me. I'm not very pretty or anything. In fact, I'm quite ugly.'

Elsie looked at her when she said that. Never in her life had she so wanted there to be an expression on her face which could show she wasn't quite sure what. Lucy moved her bishop back a square but there didn't seem any point in it. It was just something to do. She looked up at Elsie and it became a stare. It was she now who touched Elsie's hand.

'I'm sorry. I shouldn't have said that, should I? It wasn't very tactful, was it?'

'No,' said Elsie. 'I suppose it wasn't.' Lucy's hand was still there on hers.

There was nothing she was able to express. For the first time in a long while tears had come into her eyes and she frowned to make sure Lucy couldn't see them. What she wanted to express was that there was nothing on this earth she wouldn't do for Lucy. She had never in her whole life felt as much hatred as she did for Lucy's parents. She had learnt to stop hating, especially herself, before she stopped being a child. She had never felt how much she wished she could do for others. They had just been out there, not looking at her for more than a split second if they could help it. Living in a world to which she did not belong.

Lucy moved her bishop back another square, though it wasn't her turn.

'What's it like?' she asked. 'I expect it's quite horrid, actually.'

'I suppose you have to try to live for other things.'

'What other things?'

'I quite like gardens. I go on trips. And the sea. Things like that.'

'But not people so much.'

Elsie thought of her nephew and niece riding their new bicycles, of the smile on Mr Wakefield's face when she took his will to the bank. There had been other little times, helping an elderly lady with a trolley, opening a door, not every day by any means. She couldn't sound kind and friendly and thoughtful in her work and in shops and so forth with her grunting voice.

'No, not people so much.' Then she remembered her mother. 'I do have a very kind mother. I go and see her.'

'What about your father?'

'The less said about him the better.' She plonked her queen triumphantly down and said, 'Check!'

'Silly!' Lucy said, taking the queen with a pawn, of all things.

Elsie groaned and covered her face with her hands.

After a moment's uncertainty, Lucy said 'Silly!' again and giggled.

That was when Stan came back. It was a funny sight, he thought, Elsie covering her face and the girl having a laugh. He didn't know if he wanted her there. They should be keeping to themselves, not drawing attention. He stood about five yards away as they went on playing. There was something nice and settled about that.

'What are you two up to?' he asked.

Lucy beckoned him closer. 'I'm beating her at chess,' she said. The laughter was still in her voice.

'Well, I won't disturb,' he said and went on into the cottage, calling back to ask if they wanted tea. Elsie followed him into the kitchen.

'It's all right, isn't it?' she asked.

'Of course it's all right. Why shouldn't it be?' But he couldn't be sure. 'We don't want to make a habit, do we?'

There was something about the way she looked around her at nothing in particular that told him she had been made happy. 'Of course it's all right.'

'I'd better take her home. Her granny will be worried.'

They walked down the lane to Lucy's cottage. Lucy skipped on ahead. She was even singing as if nothing bad had ever happened to her. Elsie thought that Lucy probably wanted to cancel out just about everything in her life for ever. She was testing what happiness might feel like. As they approached the cottage, her grandmother came out.

The still way she stood in the doorway made her look as if she was about to be very cross. But closer up, in spite of the smile, there was only anxiety in her face. Elsie could only guess that it wasn't just because Lucy was late but because she had no idea what on earth would happen to her, what future she had, anything.

Lucy gave her a quick but strong hug. 'Sorry, Granny, we were playing chess.'

'That's nice,' her grandmother said, the fixed smile widening a little as if it had found something at last to cling onto. But the alarm remained in her eyes. 'Do come in for a moment,' she said to Elsie.

Elsie came behind them as far as the threshold. She saw a room crowded with comfortable armchairs and pictures all over the walls and ornaments and books and a real fireplace and heavy curtains. It was so homely, that was the word. She wished her mother had made a home like that, things gathered over the years and put somewhere, not arranged or lined up. Lucy had run ahead up the stairs.

'I won't stop,' Elsie said.

She couldn't stop looking at the room, how safe and comfortable it looked, and crowded with familiar things. It was somewhere for Lucy to be at peace. She wanted to say something like that, or anything to make her grandmother know that Lucy was welcome to come and see them at any time, that there were other games, that they could take her on trips, even to the sea. 'What a lovely home you have,' she said finally.

'Oh thank you!' she replied. 'It is, isn't it? Lucy's mother was brought up here after her father died. We don't quite know yet how long Lucy...'

The words seemed to catch her in her throat and she put a hand to her eyes as if the sun had suddenly come out. When she lowered it, the apologetic meekness had gone. Now, she was making it clear that her life was her business to attend to. She looked back at where Elsie could dimly see a portrait over the fireplace, of a man in a dark uniform.

'Well,' she said quite differently, as if a time had come to give a few instructions, to get a move on. 'Thank you for looking after Lucy.' She paused and looked carefully at Elsie, as though she had never really noticed her appearance before. 'Things are there to be faced, aren't they? If you're sure...'

'I really enjoyed having her, Mrs...'

'Just Isabel will do… She's a nice child, isn't she?'

Elsie knew it was enough just to nod at that.

Back at the cottage, Stan was drinking tea. He was tired, he said, having spent the best part of the day on a building site. For an instant, seeing Elsie and the girl there so happy, he had caught himself wishing this life could go on for ever: quiet days with a girl coming in from time to time to play those board games and a nice old lady next door, and Elsie, of course, just there. But it couldn't. Every time he saw a shadow at a corner, or turned suddenly, he knew that soon he would have to move on. Nothing lasted for long. He phoned his mother to say he was enjoying life in the country and that he was getting work. He didn't say where in the country. She told him she hoped he wouldn't get bored with nothing to do most of the time. Mind you, she wasn't familiar with country living herself, there was only what she'd seen on the telly which wasn't really her cup of tea.

When he put the phone down he suddenly realised how little he knew his mother, for all the ease and affection there was between them. He'd only asked her once who his father was. He'd just begun school and other children had been talking about their fathers. He'd just thought he was dead or had gone on a long journey and got stuck somewhere. She'd never mentioned him. She'd stood up quickly and gone to the kitchen, her eyes shut for a moment so that she'd had to feel for the door frame.

'Him,' she said. 'Don't you be bothering your head with things like that. I don't, so why should you?' She'd spoken in a tired, impatient way, wanting him to be sure never to raise the subject again. Anyway, it was easiest to tell people his father was dead. He stopped wondering about him after that. Now, he couldn't give a toss, the truth probably being his father didn't want to know and simply buggered off.

XIV

HENRY PHONED Dorothy one evening to say that things in Spain were 'pretty shipshape at long bloody last' and they'd be back in a couple of weeks. The time had come to put the cottage on the market again.

'Had a chance to see if it's been kept in good order for us, all that?' he asked in his brisk voice.

When they were growing up one of his favourite phases was 'Why don't you snap out of it?' For Dorothy, it was still their cottage. Their father had taken them to see it, his arms round them after he opened the door. They'd spent four holidays there. Teenage holidays, boring mainly. But the memories lingered. It had been their country home. She'd never gone there after their father had died. Why was it impossible to talk to Henry about things like memories? He and Pru, for whom everything had to be businesslike. When he spoke to her these days she couldn't help wanting to annoy him.

'I'm sure Elsie is caretaking it very well. You wouldn't have wanted it empty, would you, Henry?'

There was a pause. Perhaps Pru was on the other line.

'Well, we'll have to be the judges of that for ourselves now, won't we? Be in touch, Dorothy.'

As it turned out, Pru didn't have a view. She was beginning to have doubts about Spain, big doubts: the sort of British people it was impossible to avoid, not a word of Spanish between them, wanting her to join in this and that. Endless fancy drinks beside swimming pools. The cottage in Dorset... It was too late now. They'd sell their house too and have a flat in London.

'I'm sure Elsie has kept it beautifully,' she said. 'Seem to remember she always had a sense of beautiful things.'

'Not the best person to be showing buyers round, perhaps?' Henry replied.

She thought of some of the ghastly common people they'd met who were looking for property in Spain. 'Why on bloody earth not?' she said.

Summer was drawing to an end. Lucy often came round, sometimes with a bowl of fruit. If the weather was fine, Stan agreed not to go out to work so they could all go on a drive together. He was glad of the excuse and they didn't mind at the building site if he missed a day or two. Isabel said that that would be lovely. Twice they went to the sea. Once they went to a small safari park. There were the country houses with beautiful gardens, though they had become a bit ragged and dry and colourless-looking at the end of summer. Lucy and Elsie sat in the back of the car. Stan hardly said anything. It was their outing.

'I'm only the chauffeur,' he said once. It was the first time he'd made Elsie cross, her voice rising above a grunt.

'You're not a chauffeur,' Elsie said. 'You're our friend, isn't he, Lucy? You're the captain of our little ship.'

Lucy gave one of her little giggles, baring the metal band across her teeth. She gave Elsie her squinting look, which could make her look specially happy instead of cunning. 'I think someone can be a chauffeur and a friend,' she said.

'That's right, you tell her,' Stan said, looking at her in the driving mirror and winking.

Lucy winked one eye, then the other, as if to decide which was better. Oh dear, he thought, oh dear, there must have been other lives he could have led. He could almost imagine being Lucy's father. He wished he could imagine without disgust that Elsie was her mother too. He was ashamed of himself for having any unkind thoughts about Elsie at all. They were sitting shoulder to shoulder, pointing, getting their first glimpse of the sea as the clouds parted and the sun covered it with swathes of silver. It made him think of the photograph frame he had stolen and he was ashamed.

Usually he stayed in the car or a café while they went off on their own. He just couldn't feel like one of those tourists, wandering around gardens and such-like, pointing. Interfering with them, it would have felt, them wanting to include him. And it was true. Elsie was glad he left them alone, even though it made him seem more like a chauffeur. But today was a sea-side day. There weren't too many people about. It was too cold to sit around for long in deckchairs. They just walked along the seashore, Lucy leading the way, pick-ing up shells here and there for her grandmother, dancing in and out of the tide. Elsie walked a little way ahead of Stan, her shoes dangling from her hand. She picked up a few shells too, letting the tide run over her feet. Sometimes she caught up with Lucy squatting over a crab, perhaps, or a dead jellyfish, and they would study it together, concentrating like school-children.

Stan looked out at the horizon where a couple of ships edged along, almost obscured by the haze, or dis-tant rain. Perhaps he should really have been a seago-ing man, only coming back from time to time to this awful world, bringing money home to Elsie and Lucy, and presents from foreign ports. And visits to his mother of course, with exotic things for her nice little flat, like tablecloths and a really smart teaset. That was what he couldn't stop himself thinking when he saw Elsie and Lucy crouching down to look at something in the sand. Or watched them from a distance walking along a path in the garden of some fancy mansion or other.

Each time he glanced up at the front he thought he caught a glimpse of Ginger's brother. He was just waiting. There was the sea, grey and wrinkly and flashing when the sun came out. Like a sort of hope it was, for some. But not for him. It wasn't what he deserved, none of it, after killing a man. And then Elsie would look back at him and he knew she would have a smile on her face if she could. And he couldn't understand how she could bear to look at him like that, in the presence of that child, their happiness not touchable by anything. It was Lucy wiping a shell on her skirt, then blowing the sand out of it, then Elsie giving it a blow too, that told him they were beyond harm from him, in Elsie's eyes. And he suddenly felt what his mother used to call 'very blessed'.

It became cold as the afternoon wore on and they had tea and buns in a café. Little was said. Lucy examined her shells, which Elsie had put in her fancy floral bag.

'You'll get sand all over it,' Lucy said.

'Well, isn't that a crying shame?' Elsie replied.

Lucy liked to include Stan sometimes. 'Don't you think so, Stan,' she said, 'getting her lovely bag all mucky?'

'Knowing Elsie, she'll soon have it all cleaned up, right as rain,' he replied.

'Well, thank you, Stanley,' Elsie said.

Henry and Pru came late on the following afternoon. Elsie was pottering about, cleaning and polishing, as if she was expecting them. She saw them pause halfway up the front path, pointing. She went into the kitchen to dry a cup and saucer that were lying on the draining board. She had seen in that glimpse how much they admired the work she and Stan had done on the garden. Mid September was not a good time of year to bring out the best in gardens and they hadn't been able to enrich the soil and plant out the new shrubs until well into the summer. Still, she'd weeded the beds and cut the grass just the afternoon before and it did look attractive: the crocosmia and Japanese anemone and geraniums and buddleia all flowering. While she was weeding she had even seen a red admiral and two peacock butterflies. Perhaps there were butterflies flitting about now for Uncle Henry too.

'Well, well, well, what about that then?' he said as they turned at the door and looked back at the garden. 'Can hardly complain about that, can we?'

'No, we can't,' Pru replied. 'Bloody marvellous, actually. Added a few thou, if that's your line of thought.'

'Actually, it wasn't.' He knew she was thinking 'for a change'. He wondered if after all the hassle and expat chitter-chatter in Spain he had lost the knack of praising things just for themselves.

Elsie opened the door and stood back so they could see at once how well kept the cottage was. They had had the curtains dry-cleaned, Stan had polished the floor and painted out the drawing room and kitchen. It was spotless, beautiful. Elsie could see they were at a loss for words. Had Uncle Henry forgotten to give her a kiss? she wondered, before remembering that he never had, as though fearful of catching a disease. It was Pru who now did that, just a hand on her shoulder and a peck on her cheek.

'Would you like a cup of tea?' she said. 'I bought some nice ginger nuts and those digestives.'

They followed her into the kitchen and she could tell from Uncle Henry's mm noise that they were impressed by that too. They went back into the drawing room while the kettle boiled. She had bought some yellow roses that morning because Stan had told her how much his mother enjoyed having a flower or two in the house when he was growing up, 'to give the tidiness a touch of class', he said she'd called it. They were at the centre of the recently ironed pale blue tablecloth and the sun came out, shining directly at them and tinging the yellow with white and gold. They sat around the table, waiting for the kettle to boil. With nothing to say yet, Uncle Henry got up to look out at the window at the back. The lawn there was freshly mowed too and the small vegetable garden next to the tool shed had been freshly dug. The apples were ripening nicely on the two apple trees.

'I'm sorry, Uncle Henry,' she said. 'The lawn needs fertiliser and more topsoil and seeding. Perhaps some of it ought to be turfed. I'm sorry.'

Uncle Henry stayed at the window as the kettle came to the boil. When Elsie came back with the tea-tray and began pouring, he said, 'Elsie, I just didn't know. Your mother never told me. I'm very proud of you. I really and truly am.'

'Bloody marvellous, actually,' repeated Pru. She reached out and touched Elsie's hand. 'Well done, old thing.'

Elsie was so proud of herself that her hand shook as she gave Pru her cup of tea and handed her the plate of biscuits. She had no idea how to respond to praise. It wasn't the same when the supervisor said she'd done a satisfactory job on the hospital toilets.

'I expect it's very exotic and exciting living in Spain,' she said, 'with lovely weather all the time.'

Henry came to fetch his tea. 'Not at all bad,' he said. 'You must come and stay some time.'

'Oh yes!' Elsie said. 'I'd really love to. I really would. I've never seen another country, except on the telly, of course.'

She began to worry that Stan would be back soon. They would want to go upstairs and see that someone, a man, had been sleeping in the spare room, though she kept that spotless as well, putting his clothes away and even a vase of flowers there too, though only arti-ficial ones. There were his toothbrush and razor in the bathroom and two towels on the towel rail. Uncle Henry was saying something, not very clearly with ums and ahs, about putting the cottage on the market again, the estate agents would be bringing people round. She thought she heard Stan's car draw up.

'I must say this, Elsie, you've made it absolutely tip-top. I shall tell the agents to have another jolly good look at the price.'

They went out into the garden at the back.

'You see,' said Elsie. 'The lawn isn't very good. Those patches… We've dug out all the dandelions but…'

'So you've had a gardener in,' said Pru. 'Very wise too. Henry, there's some settling up…'

'Of course, darling, I hadn't…'

He was interrupted by the bang of the front door and a voice calling out, 'Elsie, I've got your bags of topsoil in the car…'

They went back into the drawing room to see him standing against the door. Elsie thought he did really look like a sea captain now with his big black beard speckled with grey and thick curly hair and his bared hairy arms and eyebrows which seemed thicker than she remembered. She wished she knew what to say, but it was suddenly quite easy as she went to him and said, 'Stan, I'd like you to meet my Uncle Henry and Aunt Pru. They've come to see the cottage. It belongs to them. I've only been looking after it for them while they settled themselves in Spain.'

Stan began to offer his hand but lowered it quickly when theirs remained at their sides. 'Pleased to meet you, I'm sure,' he said. There was a long pause. 'Lawn at the back needs seeing to.'

They were assuming he was a gardener and Aunt Pru was congratulating him on all the work he had done.

'No, she's the gardener. I'm just the dogsbody, just passing through.' He did not know what she'd told them. They were looking at him as if expecting him to answer a question. It was a haughty expression as though he might have ideas above his station. He'd never had dealings with people like that, people with villas in Spain and suchlike. 'I'll be back for that top-soil then,' he muttered.

Elsie knew she must spare him quickly. He looked so embarrassed, humiliated even, their not knowing who he was. Soon they would want to see the bed-rooms. She wanted them to see they had painted those too and had the curtains washed and Stan had cleaned all the windows only three days ago. When he had gone she said, 'I didn't think you'd mind, Uncle Henry. He's someone I met in the hospital. He had cancer but he's better now. He needed a short break in the country to recover his health. He was in the Royal Navy.'

She had spoken too quickly. She had never lied before. Except about Stan being a seagoing man. And to her mother to spare her feelings. Somehow being very ugly made it unnecessary to tell lies. Because nobody minded whether you told the truth or not.

'Well, he certainly seems to have done all right,'

Pru said. 'Strong as an ox by the look of it.'

Elsie waited for Uncle Henry's reply. He didn't seem pleased, and was puffing out his cheeks.

And he wasn't pleased, thinking she might bloody well have asked first, inviting any Tom, Dick or Harry for a bit of free board and lodging in the heart of the country, cancer or no cancer. Precious little sign of that. Well, what the hell did it matter now they were selling the place? Elsie might be off-putting enough but that rough-looking scoundrel... He was ashamed of himself for thinking that. Pru increasingly had to tick him off for that sort of thing. Living with expats in Spain hadn't made him more tolerant or less opinionated exactly.

'Of course not, Elsie. Between you, I've got to say it, you've done bloody wonders to the place, pardon my Spanish...' Pru was giving him one of her looks and tapped her breast. 'Now look...'

He sat down at the table and took out his cheque-book. Not a chance Pru would accuse him of being stingy this time. He wrote out a cheque for a thousand pounds. 'There you are, Elsie dear. For doing a wonderful caretaking job and all the expenses there must have been. I'm very proud of you. I didn't know...'

Elsie knew what he might have been about to say. 'I didn't know you had it in you.' He didn't know anything about her at all, just a cleaner in some hospital, poor old thing. Pru caught a glimpse of the cheque and gave a brief nod. Henry glanced out of the window and saw Stan carrying bags of topsoil to the bottom of the garden and dumping them next to the shed.

'Useful-looking chap,' he said.

Elsie didn't want her uncle to talk about Stan like that. He was the only man she'd known at all closely. Some of the cleaners were men but they usually came from other countries and could hardly speak English. They were always quiet and thoughtful, thinking about home a long way away.

It was all coming to an end soon. She watched Stan tip the bags of soil off his shoulder. She could not imagine life without him now. She knew he liked her; well, he was grateful to her. As he walked back round the side of the cottage with that swagger of his, she wondered if it was something like this to be in love with someone, waiting for their return. The cheque lay in front of her and she hadn't even said thank you for it.

'Oh please, Uncle Henry! You don't really, you needn't…'

'Oh yes, he does,' Pru said.

They went to see the bedrooms, up the polished stairs, past another vase of flowers on the landing. Uncle Henry just said, 'Gosh! Perfect, Elsie! Someone's going to jump at this place.'

Downstairs, they said they had to get on. They were staying with a friend in Swanage and hoped to fit in a game of golf the following morning, then 'back to our Spanish hideaway', Uncle Henry said.

'The agents will be in touch.'

'The more's the pity,' Aunt Pru muttered, again touching Elsie's shoulder and kissing her lightly on the cheek.

This time Uncle Henry kissed her too, laying his hand lightly on her back. 'Thanks, Elsie,' he said. He saw Stan coming down the path with more topsoil. 'And thanks to your chum too. Quite a team.'

Stan passed them with a raise of his hand.

Elsie waved and thought that was what they were, a team. And it was all coming to an end. People would come and one day soon an offer would be made and the future would start all over again.

At the gate Henry said to Pru, 'Well, what about that then?'

But she wasn't there. She had gone back and was talking to Elsie in the doorway. Elsie was gripping her arm and vigorously nodding. When she came back he said, 'So what was all that about?'

'I've invited her to Spain. Told her to get a passport. Given her dates. She was thrilled.'

'I see.'

Elsie and Stan talked about it that evening over supper, but not much. There wasn't much to say, a world ending and an unknown world beginning. Elsie said she'd go back to London and Stan said he'd stay down in that neck of the woods. He would finish his training as a gas-fitter, find a nice little place, 'not as nice as this though, not by a long chalk'.

Elsie thought then about Lucy and that became the worst. It was like a family breaking up, all those little expeditions coming to an end. And not knowing what would happen to her. They were taking her to the seaside again tomorrow and she was so excited about that, about gathering more shells for her granny who was making a sort of tray with them.

'Another trip to the seaside tomorrow, Stan.'

'I'll look forward to that. Nice kid, that Lucy. Makes me feel young again. As if nothing had happened, if you get my meaning.'

He was looking at her as if searching her face for something, as if he wanted to be sure she understood what he was talking about, what happiness there might have been. She knew perfectly well what he meant.

'Perhaps she can be happy too one day,' was the best she could think of.

XV

IT WAS THE best day ever. There was hardly anyone on the beach with the schools having opened. A day in early September when the wind blew clouds across the sun and just when you thought it was getting cold, the sun came out again, blazing forth as if making up for lost time. Stan came with them to the beach again, walking some way behind as they gathered shells and skipped in and out of the rising tide. Lucy's laugh was full of moments of sudden delight. Elsie laughed too but it was more like clearing her throat. She had brought a tea towel to carry the shells in. Once they found a pool and when he caught up with them they were on their hands and knees, searching in the seaweed for cockles and lifting little creatures in the palms of their hands. He walked on and, turning back, saw Elsie tending to a scratch on Lucy's knee and binding a handkerchief round it. Their heads were touching. He was too far away to hear what they were saying. He walked further on to a rock where he sat and stared out at the sea, all glittering one moment, wrinkled and grey the next, as the clouds sped across the sun. He wished the wind could sweep him away to some quiet place, sheltered from storms and sunlight, a quiet, small place where he could become someone else, a real seagoing man coming home and settling down after a lifetime's journeying, his boat moored in some forgotten harbour and allowed to rust. Staring out at the sea, he only wished he wasn't what he had been, the past always lurking there over his shoulder. There were Lucy and Elsie in the distance, back at the pool now, as if that was what happiness might look like, to be remembered or looked forward to, not just the bloody big windswept blank of the sea like the years to come...

When they stood up to follow Stan, Lucy said,

'I've got a secret to tell you.'

The sun caught the band across her teeth. Elsie could tell it was a happy secret. There had been no real happiness up to then. Collecting shells and skipping in and out of the water were only things to be done now, to forget what there wasn't to look forward to or what had happened and gone on happening. Every time she looked at Lucy she could guess that there were noises in her head, terrible angry noises that she was trying to shut her ears to. She was trying not to think about where she would go next, as if the doors of her life behind and before her were always swinging open on the darkness beyond. Elsie remembered she had learnt that soon, to keep the doors shut, and now they opened wide on beautiful gardens in all the seasons, so that what was happening now could seem to go on for ever, garden after garden till the end of time. She waited for Lucy to tell her about the surprise.

'My mummy's coming tomorrow. She's actually coming to stay and we're going to find somewhere to live not far from granny.'

What was the right question to ask? Was everything going to start being all right? And her father? What would the arrangement be? Would the quarrelling stop? She wanted to know everything, how happy Lucy might become. But that wasn't it. It was the end. Her mother would take her away. The estate agents would start bringing people to look around. And there was Stan walking ahead again, as if to leave them behind, not looking back, as if he'd walk round the headland and they'd never set eyes on him again.

'You don't seem very pleased exactly,' Lucy was saying.

Elsie touched her shoulder. 'Of course I'm pleased.'

And she knew that because of her gruff voice, Lucy could not tell if she really was.

They walked back along the beach. The tea towel was full of shells. They let the tide wash over their feet. The clouds had thickened and now the sea was only lit dimly in the distance. The wind was scattering the spray as if rain had come. Stan was waiting for them at the car. He said it was getting cold and he would drive them to a café. As they drove off, Elsie said,

'Wonderful news, Stan. Lucy's mother coming tomorrow.'

'That'll be nice for you then,' he said, glancing at her in the driving mirror. She had a big glinting smile on her face, from ear to ear.

Elsie looked down at Lucy, who had turned to stare out of the window. The smile seemed to have gone. Her future had started again to be thoughtful about and she and Stan might already be people she'd known once a long time ago.

It was then that Stan glanced again in his mirror and thought he saw Johnny Boyd in the distance, leaning against a car and giving him a wave, then drawing a hand across his throat.

That evening they hardly spoke. Elsie had taken Lucy home.

'I've heard the good news,' she said.

The old woman did not have that fixed smile, now that she had something to smile about. She held Lucy tight against her. She had no intention of saying anything, her hands clasped across Lucy's chest. She was waiting for Lucy to say what she did say.

'Thank you, Elsie, it was a really lovely afternoon.'

'Yes, it was,' Elsie replied.

The old woman held Lucy even tighter, clinging onto her. She bit her lip, as if not trusting herself to speak, even to smile, as if that might be to take a chance too many.

Elsie suddenly remembered the first time they went to the sea and found a dead seagull. Its eye was wide open and it had an angry look as if it was about to leap up into their faces.

Lucy stood back. 'It's got oil on its wings,' she said too loudly.

Stan came up behind them. 'Poor little sod,' he said. 'Won't want to go on lying there being gawped at. You go on. I'll see to that.'

They walked on, not speaking. Twice Elsie looked back. The first time she saw Stan carrying the bird up the beach. The second time he was digging a deep hole in the sand with a piece of driftwood. He wouldn't want just to cover it up, she thought.

'He's burying it,' she said.

'It died because it couldn't fly,' Lucy said, pointing at the sky becoming blue above the sea.

It was the first time Elsie touched Lucy, laying a hand for an instant on her shoulder. It was only instead of having to think of anything to add. Then Lucy stooped to pick up another shell. Stan still kept his distance from them, perhaps wanting to see them like that, like someone's family.

The first people came to look at the cottage two

days later. The agent showed them round. Elsie might just as well not have been there. She wasn't even introduced. She was hardly looked at. Once or twice the agent almost brushed her aside if she was getting in the way.

On the fourth day a couple were looking around when Stan came home. He closed the door quietly behind him and stared at the agent, who was pointing down the garden and saying something about the tool shed. From his voice, Stan thought, he might almost have been pleading for his life. Elsie was in the kitchen doorway and glanced at him with a shrug. He could tell she had been ignored. The agent began rubbing his hands. 'Let's just have a look at the upstairs, shall we?' he was saying. He didn't ask Elsie if she would mind that. Then he saw Stan, who had moved towards the foot of the stairs.

'Ah!' he said.

'We don't mind them having a look upstairs, do we, Elsie?'

Elsie gave her gruff chuckle. 'No, Stanley, I think I can rightly say we have no overriding objection to that.'

She had no idea where that phrase came from. She often overheard people saying things to make them feel more important. Sometimes she even tried them out. The couple looked at Stan, who was not making way for them. They were exchanging glances as the agent began to say something. Stan put out his hand

and the agent took it. The couple offered their hands too.

'It's a delightful place you have here,' the man said, glancing at the agent for an explanation.

'Stanley and Elsie,' Stan said. 'Now they must feel free, mustn't they, Elsie? We have no objection, do we?'

He turned to the agent, who had begun to stammer, 'Of course, of course, of course…'

Stan made way for them and they went up the stairs. And then, she didn't know why, Elsie went up to him and put her arms round him and laid her cheek on his chest.

'It's our home, isn't it? Who do those people think they are? They said they might build a porch and buy a summer house instead of the tool shed. They said they might knock down the kitchen wall. They said…'

Stan pushed her away. 'A cuppa, I think, Elsie.'

The couple and the agent spent a long time upstairs, talking, walking up and down, making plans. The agent returned on his own. He stood in the kitchen doorway.

'Leave them to it,' he said. He was trying to sound much older than he was, not on the buyers' side any longer. His fringe was covering one eye and he straightened his tie. Then he gripped his lapel as if on the verge of an announcement. 'Clive Fairhust,' he said. 'I'm sorry to have caused you any inconvenience.'

The couple were coming back down the stairs. 'Ah, there we are!'

He spread his arm to steer them to the door. They stood on the threshold for a last look, nodded at each other. The agent was smiling. He knew he had made a sale. As they left, the man raised his hand and the woman stared. When they next came back they would not expect to find them there, in a house that wasn't theirs. That was the look on their faces: Never want to set eyes on you again, frankly.

As the door closed behind them, Elsie heard the agent say, 'Oh yes, madam, absolutely, full vacant possession... Tomorrow...'

It did not take long. Dorothy told Elsie the following evening that an offer had been made and would be accepted.

'So you'll have to move out soon. Won't you, dear? You and your friend. Ten days maximum, Uncle Henry said.'

It was the way Henry had spoken about Elsie being there, saying she'd kept it very nice but all the same... She hadn't lost her temper with him for a long time, not since he'd put those ridiculous prices on their father's furniture.

'Frankly, Henry, I think you should be very grateful to Elsie, not just kick her out.'

'Temper, temper! I am grateful. Gave her a whopping great cheque, if you must know. Two weeks then.' He put the phone down with a deep sigh.

Dorothy asked Elsie what she would do. Elsie said she would return to her flat and carry on as before. It was such a silly question.

'What else can I do, Mother?' There was no reply. 'And there are lots of my sort of job.'

'Of course, dear. Of course there are.'

When she put the phone down, Stan said he had a call to make. He didn't mind any longer if Elsie overheard him. Soon he'd be seeing the last of her. He looked at her as if she was a stranger again, like when they'd first met on the bus and he'd told her he'd killed a man – just to stop her bloody staring at him. An ugly stranger. He didn't want to go on feeling so grateful to her, now that he had to move on.

He phoned to ask what the latest was about Ginger's brother. His friend made it clear that Badger couldn't be bothered with too much of that history lark. Anyway, he wasn't around much, spending most of his time in Spain. 'Call it a day, Stan, that's my frank advice. I told Badger you'd called the last time and he couldn't remember at first who you were: "Stan who?" he said.'

'I've got to know,' Stan said. 'I thought I saw him.'

'Maybe you did. Maybe you didn't. He's a fucking wreck, to be frank. Hospital. Drink. Operations. That kind of thing. You know what Badger said. He said, 'It comes to us all in the fullness of time, the dying of the light.' Always had a way with words, did Badger.'

No one would know where he went on to now.

There were rooms to rent, there were building jobs, he'd finish his gas training, any bloody thing really. Go and see his mum, of course. She'd told him she was in fine fettle, there were friends and the telly and the bingo and things: 'What more could I want but my nice little home?' As soon as he was settled he'd go and see her again. 'I have my memories,' she said. 'There's that nice photo of you the day you left school.' She'd never made him feel guilty he didn't see her more often. She wanted him to know she felt contented with life.

After the call from Dorothy, Lucy came round with her mother. Elsie hadn't seen her for days.

She had seen her granny at the shop who told her they'd gone on a little holiday together. That smile was back but now it came and went, sure of itself. The sun came out as they left the shop and it caught the weathervane on the church, making them both look up at it, as though it had been struck by lightning.

'You've been very kind to Lucy,' her grandmother said.

How could Elsie ever explain that it was Lucy who had been kind to them, just being there.

'Teaching me to be better at chess, that's what she's done.' It sounded so silly, said in that gruff voice, her face blank.

'She told me…and all those lovely shells. Oh dear, oh dear. Life's a funny old thing.'

Lucy stood in front of her mother. They were so alike, their broad mouths and their hair the same dark blonde, uncombed and falling about their faces, and their eyes keeping no secrets, just hoping for the best and wanting to go on being happy. It was how Elsie had always wanted to be. How could such a gentle-looking woman shout and be shouted at? Where did hatred come from, like something swooping out of the dark and seizing you by the throat? She had decided to stop hating a long time ago. Sometimes the gardens were near to churches and she went into them and even knelt, staring up at the altar, so as to imagine herself as one of the thousands who had gone before. She had been taught how to pray. Her mother had sent her to Sunday school and they had gone to morning service together, her mother singing on and off with her thin piping voice, and she had wanted to sing. But her voice was a growl and she could only hum, a deep hum as she mouthed the words and her mother smiled down at her, as if to say that God would be pleased she was making the effort. There was no hatred in those places. What else could she think, looking at Lucy and her mother, as if they had broken free of what had once possessed them? While they stood there in that moment or two she had been praying for them...

'We've come to say goodbye,' Lucy's mother said. It was a voice that could never be raised and yet Lucy had heard it differently. They had been separated from themselves and now...

'And to say thank you very much,' Lucy added. She had become too happy to mind saying goodbye, perhaps for ever. She was in a hurry for what would happen next. Her mouth closed firmly over her teeth. She wanted to be serious and correct.

'Won't you come in?' Elsie asked.

Lucy's mother shook her head. Her hands now rested on Lucy's shoulders and she gave them a squeeze. Her eyes became suspicious for an instant, even frightened, and she closed them with a frown as if to stop herself from seeing something.

'We're going to Cornwall. I have a friend there who can put us up. She has a daughter of Lucy's age. They can go to school together. Perhaps we will stay there. You'd like that, wouldn't you, darling?'

Lucy nodded and then they were turning to go. Elsie was nodding too. 'I hope you will be very happy,' she said. Then she added hurriedly because it seemed the most important thing, that they weren't being left behind, wouldn't be lonely without them. 'The cottage is being sold. We will soon be leaving too.'

Lucy showed no surprise but her mother said 'Oh!' She hesitated. 'I'm sorry.' Then she hurried Lucy away, as if they had come to the wrong place.

They did not turn back for a final wave at the gate. Elsie went back into the cottage and sat on the sofa for a long time. She closed her eyes and found she was praying. She wanted to stop feeling sorry for herself. Later she went up to her room and lay on her bed. She thought of Lucy's mother, that kind, open, untroubled face distorted by fury. She did not hear Lucy return and leave something on the doorstep.

It was a wooden box inlaid with seashells. Inside it was a silver and blue ballpoint pen with a little fleet of yachts painted on it. The letter said: Dear Elsie and Captain Stan. Thank you for being kind to me. I shall never forget you. I think we both need to improve our chess if the truth were known. These aren't the shells we collected of course which I'm making into something else for granny. It's quite easy to get spare cartridges for the pen, Stan. Lots of love, Lucy.

The buyers came the next day to do some measuring. They did not ask for permission. When Elsie offered them tea they barely responded, as if they had already forgotten who she was, the future in their new home having become so exciting. When they had gone Elsie went into the lane and saw Lucy and her mother loading suitcases into a car. She could hear them faintly chattering away. The old lady stood in the doorway. Elsie tried to imagine her sadness too and would have liked to have been standing there beside her, getting ready to wave. She went back down the path to the village shop to buy their supper. She would buy a Fisherman's Pie, which was one of Stan's favourites, saying it took him back to the old days when he steered his boat back to harbour from the stormy deep.

XVI

WHEN SHE returned, the car had gone from outside Lucy's granny's house. On the way back she had noticed another car that had been reversed onto the grass verge and into the edge of the wood. Sometimes she had seen lovers there coming back to their cars, hand in hand and grinning.

She had not locked the door. When she opened it she saw a man facing her across the table. He had his hands under a newspaper in front of him. He was leaning forward, staring at her. She had never seen such colourless eyes. It was as if he was blind. But at the same time they had anger in them, a defeated, desperate anger. Strands of ginger hair brushed across his head had straggled loose down to his eyes. His forehead was covered in little scabs, some of them spotted with blood. His face was white as milk and glistened with sweat. From the quivering of his jaw, Elsie could tell he was gritting his teeth. She did not expect him to speak. Then he cleared his throat.

'Seen you from a distance. Scraping the bottom of the fucking barrel is our Stanley.' His voice was squeaky as if begging for something.

'Stan won't be back for a while,' she said. He wouldn't tell from her voice how frightened she was.

'I can wait. I know when he comes back, darling.'

She wanted to be very polite, to pretend she did not know why he was there. 'I'll just take the shopping into the kitchen,' she said, then added, 'Would you care for a cup of tea, by any chance?'

The anger burst out of him and his voice became squeakier. 'Got you where he wants you, skivvying. It takes all fucking sorts.' His voice was now slurred and his eyes swivelled across her as she went into the kitchen. She asked again if he would like a cup of tea.

'I don't think a cup of tea is what I'm after, thank you,' he said, as if suddenly remembering his manners. 'Not at this moment.'

Stan could be back at any time. She listened for his car. She fumbled with the bread and Fisherman's Pie and butter as she put them into the fridge. She had forgotten she'd bought eggs and heard them break as she dropped the shopping bag. She knew what to do. Stan kept his gun at the back of the second drawer behind the cutlery. She'd asked him to hide it some-where else, perhaps in the tool shed. Once she had found him cleaning it and saw the bullets in it. 'No point in having something that doesn't work, is there?' He'd told her never to touch it. He'd pointed at a switch pushed forward. 'Ready to fire,' he'd told her.

She glanced through to the drawing room where the man was leaning further forward, his hand fiddling under the newspaper. She thought she heard the sound of a car. It was too early for Stanley. Perhaps it was Lucy leaving with her mother, at the start of their long journey to Cornwall. It was so easy to imagine them, Lucy chattering away, her mother's silence, listening, nodding but remembering too, travelling off into a new life.

There was no hesitation in her, no doubt, as if all her life she had wanted to know for sure there was a thing to be done. She took the gun and hid it under a tea cloth and went back. It was definitely the sound of Stan's car. She could see the man's concentration, the widening of his eyes, the stiffening of his hands under the newspaper.

'I've just got to see to the...' she began, but she had no story. She had no idea why she might be wandering behind him with a tea towel over her hands. She heard the click of the front gate.

'Just you fuck off out of here, you ugly fucking bitch,' he muttered.

She raised the gun and closed her eyes and pulled the trigger. The explosion was a huge crash inside her head. She could not look, screwing up her eyes, letting the gun drop and falling to her knees. She covered her face with her hands and began sobbing.

Stan was kneeling beside her. He had his hand on her back, then round her shoulder. His voice was very slow and very gentle. 'It's all right. It's Captain Pugwash here. Now listen to me carefully.'

She looked up at him between her fingers. Her sobbing had nearly stopped. His face was very close and he gave her a wink. She couldn't help trying to smile. She caught a glimpse of the body lying beside the table and the fallen chair. Stan was talking.

'All you do, my darling, is this. You make yourself a nice cup of tea and go up to your room and lie down with a magazine and soon everything will be right as rain. I'm not a seagoing man for nothing.'

He lifted her to her feet and, holding her tightly, led her into the kitchen, standing beside her while she made a cup of tea, then put his arm round her again and led her to the foot of the stairs. He followed her and saw her to the door of her bedroom, giving her the thumbs-up sign as she lay down, wiping the last of the tears from her face.

'I'll be in for my supper later,' he said.

'I got us Fisherman's Pie,' she muttered.

'That's my lovely Elsie,' he said.

He fetched a blanket from his room, went back down the stairs and covered the body with it, after taking a bunch of keys from the jacket pocket. There was a pool of blood spreading over the wooden floor. He dropped the two guns into the plastic bag, which he put beside the door leading to the back garden. He had known exactly what he had to do the moment he came into the cottage after hearing the shot and saw the body lying there and Elsie kneeling and sobbing beyond it. In all his life he had never known anything so simple. Not since his mother had told him when he left school to get a good job with a pension and keep his nose clean and always keep up appearances. It was simple, knowing that all he had to do with his life was to make his mother happy.

He tucked the blanket under the body, then rolled it over, quickly covering the face, but he caught a glimpse of it, the gaping mouth, an eye still open. Wrapping the blanket round it, he dragged the body down to the bottom of the garden and laid it beside the tool shed. The bags of topsoil were laid in a row on the far side of the vegetable plot. They had tried to grow vegetables and there was a row of carrots waiting to be pulled up and two rows of cabbages that were going to seed. They'd only eaten two cabbages and agreed they weren't as tasty as the ones from the supermarket. There was a cluster of spring onions which neither of them fancied much. All the vegetables were waiting to be removed and thrown away.

He remembered finding a pickaxe when they first looked into the tool-shed. 'Everything including a bloody pickaxe,' he'd said to Elsie. He took it and a sharp spade and began lifting the earth and digging. He wondered if the sound could be heard from Lucy's grandmother's cottage. He wondered what she'd thought when she heard the shot. There had sometimes been shots in the wood and Elsie said it was probably rabbits or even foxes now that they couldn't be hunted any longer. Or birds like pheasants. They laughed once about how little they knew about life in the countryside. There was no one they wanted to ask. People might wonder why such an odd couple were living there at all without them asking a lot of obvious questions.

He did not finish until long after dark. A full moon floated out from a pure white cloud as he rolled the body into the hole. He fetched the plastic bag with the guns in it and dropped it on top of the body. Then he filled the hole, stamped the earth flat, pulled up the rest of the vegetables and spread the soil evenly with a rake. The moon was now in a clear sky, shining down on the earth. And he thought how ready, how prepared it looked for new planting. Perhaps the new owners would plant flowers there. That was what Elsie had wanted, listing flowers they could grow and cut and put in vases around the house. But in the end they'd left it as it was, with vegetables sown by others.

'Where's the Fisherman's Pie then?' he called up the stairs. It was then he remembered the bloodstain, the trail of blood there might have been to the door leading to the garden. But there was no blood. He looked where the stain had been and the wood shone. He could smell floor polish. She had come down to see to that, dear Elsie. There were tears in his eyes, on the verge of spilling out, as she came down the stairs. He blew his nose.

'Just give my hands a good wash and have a nice bath,' he said. Almost every time he washed his hands he remembered his mother making sure that was something he never forgot.

When he came back, the Fisherman's Pie was waiting for him with some baked beans.

'Can I do you an egg?' she asked.

'What are you having?' he asked.

He wished, he had always wished, he could tell from that face what she was thinking. Her voice had been steady. There was no point telling her what he had been doing. He could not bring himself to thank her for saving his life, perhaps both their lives. And only now, as he took his first mouthful of Fisherman's Pie, did he realise that when he heard the shot and ran from the car to the gate and up the front path, it was because he had to know what harm she must have come to, and that whatever it was was waiting for him too. He could tell nothing from her face, nothing, except this: that both understood they had risked their lives for each other. He couldn't stop staring at her. He laid his hand on hers, squeezed it, and she did then smile, a snarl, a grimace that understanding shone through. She turned her hand up and gripped his very quickly and he finished his Fisherman's Pie.

'You look like you enjoyed that, Captain,' she said.

'It wasn't bad. I've caught the odd bit of fish in my time.'

There was the rest of the business to be done.

'I won't hang about, Elsie,' he said, taking out the car keys. 'There's a car to be disposed of. Might be back late tomorrow.'

And he left with another wink and she raised a hand to him. A few moments later she heard a car drive off. There was nothing to do but wash up and watch a bit of television. Warfare. All the suffering. Troubled families. Great kindness here and there, the standard set as she'd often observed in hospitals. And great greed too and an emptiness of mind beyond stupidity among people thrown together in a house... It was all coming to an end. The agent would soon come for the keys. Stan would drive her to a railway station. They would say goodbye. They would promise to keep in touch. It was strange, knowing a man like Stan who owed you everything, who might want to tell you that. She didn't even know if he was a good man. Except that he sometimes spoke about his mother, how he'd go on trying to keep it in mind never to let her down.

The agent phoned the following morning to say he'd pick up the keys in two days, 'if that was all right'. She said it was. She began tidying the cottage up, wiping and dusting, so that it was shipshape everywhere. She even did a bit of touching-up with paint in the kitchen and downstairs toilet. She gave the floor another waxing and polishing. She walked halfway down the garden and saw the fresh dark brown square of soil. For a moment she thought she saw it move and hurried back into the house and sat down, hugging herself and trembling. Stan came back late on the following evening.

'All done and dusted,' he said.

She did not ask where he'd gone, not at first. But he knew she expected him to tell her. 'I'm sorry to be boring,' she said. 'But it's Fisherman's Pie again. There's peas too this time.'

What she was not telling him was whether she had gone to the bottom of the garden to where the vegetables had been and the soil was raked flat and the grass and weeds would soon begin to grow.

He took a big mouthful. 'I had to get rid of his car, didn't I? Leave it quite a long way away. Bloody awful rattle-trap it was, I can tell you. Lucky to get further than the main road.' She was watching him enjoy his Fisherman's Pie. 'And so what have you been up to?'

She said she'd been tidying up, even doing a bit of touching-up with white matt emulsion. 'I just had a quick look,' she said.

'We've got a day or two to enjoy ourselves,' he said.

The following afternoon, Elsie called on Lucy's granny. She was invited in and sat on the edge of an armchair, looking around the room while Isabel fetched a glass of orangeade. There were two large portraits of men in naval uniform and the room was packed with old-looking ornaments and objects, each one of which she wanted to ask a question about. She had surrounded herself with the whole of her past, as though every single thing was there to remind her, to make sure she wouldn't start forgetting anything. She could reach out and touch this or that, as if making time stand still.

There was no permanent smile now. She just looked tired. Perhaps her afternoon nap had been interrupted and she just wanted to doze there surrounded by her things.

'It is rather crowded, isn't it? I'm just not very good at throwing things away, I'm afraid.'

'I just wanted to know that Lucy and her mother got off safely,' Elsie said. Isabel only nodded, perhaps not wanting a conversation to begin to interrupt memories. 'We did enjoy meeting her,' Elsie added, then remembered the other reason she had come, 'The cottage has been sold and we'll be moving out early next week.'

There was still no response. 'I thought you would like to know.'

Isabel looked around the room, as if for the last time, seizing hold of it. 'I shall miss you. I hope my new neighbours are as nice as you are. I wish I had got to know you better. I come from a naval family. The sea is in my blood, as they say. I would have liked to have talked about it to your friend Stanley.'

There had been something dismissive in her voice. Elsie got up to go. She then saw the round table by the window where all Lucy's shells had been laid out. 'Oh look!' she said.

'Yes,' was all Isabel replied at first, then added, 'a memory of Lucy, to add to the others.'

They wanted to make something of the end of their time together. Elsie said she would just go back to her flat and Stan said he'd run her to the station. He told Elsie that he would go and see his mother but he couldn't stay up there. He could tell her now that he didn't like people pointing at him, knowing she would understand. She'd asked him once if his mother minded that, being pointed at herself. 'You don't know my Mum,' he said.

They decided they would visit a famous garden and then go on to have a last look at the sea. 'I've got a taste for it, if the truth were known,' he said. 'There's work down here. There's a gas-fitting course I can do, part two of my NVQ.'

And still they said nothing about what had happened, only that they must keep in touch. It was Stan who had to suggest this. Elsie could not say it herself because Stan only wanted to forget everything except his mother. He was the opposite of Isabel, never wanting to stop being reminded. He had her address if he wanted to write to her.

The garden they visited wasn't at its best now that

it was early September. Elsie pointed at the plants and trees and flowers, giving them their names. There was a shower when they had to shelter in a hut which looked out on two long herbaceous borders. They looked bedraggled and dim until the sun suddenly came out and it was as if everything was about to burst into flower. The people started walking slowly around again, shaking the rain out of their umbrellas. They were thinking the same. There they were, strangers to one another, strolling around gardens, pointing, admiring, filling their minds with the variable loveliness, the blossoming and fading of things. While in their own minds Elsie and Stan were seeing a body slumped beside a table, rolled into a pit and covered over with earth. They were hearing the shot of a gun. And they were feeling what the other people could not feel, another kind of happiness; they could not help it. They were trying to persuade themselves that an evil, a horror, had been done away with, that they had not just been saving their own lives, wanting the garden to seem as glorious to them as to all the others.

'Now for the sea,' Stan said.

They had it almost to themselves. It was where they had once gone with Lucy. Elsie gathered a few shells, then remembered and threw them away. With hardly any wind, the water gleamed flat under a grey sky. There were four ships moving along the horizon.

'I wonder where they're bound for,' Stan said loudly, as if the quiet sea was making too much noise, sloshing along the shore.

'I do too,' said Elsie. 'I really do. I would like to see them unload and follow the loads until they are unpacked in warehouses and become things sold in shops, perhaps.'

'We are the philosopher today, aren't we?'

He picked up a shell and threw it far into the sea. 'Good old Lucy, she'd have liked that one,' he said, looking down and back at her, as she tried to keep up with him. 'Good old Elsie too while I'm about it.'

They walked a long way. They did not want this day to end. They hardly noticed the one or two people who had a good look at them before changing direction up the beach, calling their dogs, as if out of harm's way. They turned back.

'So Fisherman's Pie again tonight, is it?' he asked.

'Wait and see,' she replied, though she had no idea yet what she would cook for supper.

XVII

THEY STOPPED at the estate agent's to drop off the keys on the way to the station. The people who had bought the cottage had come the previous afternoon. They did some more measuring and twice wanted it confirmed that the keys would be handed over the next day. Stan and Elsie waited for them on the patio looking out over the garden. The people asked to see the tool shed and Stan took them there. He had tidied it thoroughly, with all the tools lined up and hanging from hooks. He had oiled the lawnmower. He showed them the shelf with grass seed and fertiliser and moss-killer and insecticide, all lined up too. The household tools were kept there as well. The couple looked down at the vegetable patch.

'Was a bit of a mess,' Stan said. 'Dug up all the veg, all ready for the next season.'

'Very nice,' the man said.

They pointed at it, lowering their voices. 'Not really vegetable people,' the woman said, 'are we?'

'Just the place,' the man said, rubbing his hands. 'Can't wait.'

Elsie watched them come back down the garden. The last time she'd sat there she'd played chess with Lucy. She remembered vividly her wide smile with the band gleaming across her teeth, the big eager eyes, as though playing chess was the most exciting thing in the world, so much better than everything that had gone before. She saw the couple to the door. They looked around them, not with excitement but as if to say that that would have to do for the time being. They had measured the floors and windows. It was the décor that was not to their liking. Elsie hoped they might say something favourable before they left.

'Perfect,' the man said. He paused for a long time. 'Thank you.'

'Come along,' the woman said.

They had walked down the path. They did not turn round. There wasn't even a lifting of the hand.

Stan did not see her to the platform because there was no parking at the station. He took out her suitcase and fetched a trolley. They stood there and he put his arms round her, pressing her head for a moment against his chest.

'Not goodbye,' he said. 'Au revoir.' That was what his mother always said, as if she had just come across a fancy new idea in a fancy new language.

'You'll have to send me your address,' she said.

'I've got yours,' he said.

'I can send you postcards of some of those gardens.'

'That would be nice. Off you go then. The train's this side. You don't have to cross the bridge or anything.'

They had separated. She had her hands on the trolley. 'I'll be off then.'

She turned once and waved. He raised his hand and blew her a kiss. She walked a little way down the platform. She was crying so much she had to sit down on a bench. The trolley was in the way of people going to the end of the platform.

'Goodbye, Stan,' she murmured, blowing her nose hard to pull herself together. It was just as it had been when she cried as a child. Her mother seizing her nose in a handkerchief and saying, 'Blow!' The dead man was still waiting for her along the side of her mind, staring but dimming now and further away.

Her flat needed a good dusting and wiping and hoovering but it was soon as if she had never left it. She decided to change the postcards of gardens in the big frames she had bought at the framing shop. It would help to make a new start. There were one or two things she could do, even change the curtains with the money Uncle Henry had given her. She rang the agency and was told there were plenty of hospital cleaning jobs going. When could she start? They sounded pleased to hear from her. The following day she would go and see her mother. Normal life was going on again. Except now she would be waiting to hear from Stan. Except now there was what had happened so she could never be quite calm again, just mopping and wiping and visiting gardens and being hastily stared at. It had been terrible but she was proud of herself too. She couldn't help it. She had never known what it was to be proud of herself before, not even when the supervisor had said she'd done a good job cleaning in the hospital. That had happened twice. It was as if these two feelings grappled with each other behind the surface of life, leaving her free to get on with it. They were becoming none of her business. She hoped she would not seem different to her mother. As always, it only mattered that she would not worry about her.

Dorothy seemed glad to see her and wanted to know all about the cottage. There was Lucy and her grandmother to tell her about. And the garden, of course. And the new owners.

'What about your friend?' Dorothy asked.

'Oh, he made a complete recovery.'

'Tell me about him.'

'He was a seaman until his health deteriorated.'

'What sort of a seaman?'

'Mainly in the deep-sea fishing industry.'

'There are many problems in that walk of life nowadays. With overfishing and things like that.'

'I know. He told me all about it.'

There was a pause. Dorothy got up and walked to the window. 'I have some sad news to tell you,' she said. 'Your father died.'

Elsie had never told her she'd been to see him in his seaside bungalow. She thought it might be disloyal. She didn't want to have to say anything about the not very nice woman at all he'd left her for. She just sat there, remembering him, the noises in the background, the sadness that nothing had worked out particularly well and the things that had begun to go wrong with him. She just sat and muttered that she was sorry.

'Of course, dear, you barely knew him, did you? You didn't know him at all.'

'What did Geoffrey think? Did Geoffrey ever go and see him?'

'Not to my knowledge. He just said "Oh!" actually.'

'There's another thing. His will. It isn't much but when she dies the proceeds of the bungalow go to you two. She's pretty sick, I gather. It's not a lot with the remaining mortgage but better than a kick in the teeth, as my father used to say.'

She turned. 'You don't look particularly pleased.'

But Elsie was only hoping the woman would die quite soon and then she could give a little something to Stan to help him on the way in his new life. She'd be able to visit gardens to her heart's content. She could help one or two of the foreign cleaners to go home to see their loved ones. Her mother had once paid for her to learn to drive and she could buy a little car.

'After all, he should have left it to you, shouldn't he?'

Dorothy laughed. 'Dear, dear Elsie!'

Stan had already found a room to rent near his building job. He could continue his NVQ training no more than ten miles away. After two weeks he went to see his flat. It was as he had last seen it, things strewn everywhere, the ripped bedding and curtains and smashed television and broken chairs. There was nothing to salvage. On the stairs the two other occupants were arguing about the kitchen as though they'd been at it ever since. They hardly noticed him. He spoke to his landlord and told him he was leaving. He'd been away and someone had trashed the place. His rent had been paid in advance and anything else could be covered by his deposit. He looked around it for the last time and smiled. 'Come and look for me now,' he said.

His mother had not expected him. He said he'd moved on from that cottage and wanted to stay in the south. Perhaps one day he could find a nice place where they could be together. He suddenly realised how old she was getting, shifting about in her chair as if that was movement enough.

'No, Stanley, I couldn't. I've got my friends. And this flat. Well, I've built it up little by little over the years, haven't I?'

He nodded. Did he have to explain to her yet again he couldn't live up there near to her, with people pointing and knowing who he was? Of course he didn't.

'I'll come and see you often,' he said.

'I always enjoy your visits.' She shifted again in her chair. 'That beard of yours. Is it a fixture?'

'Don't you like it?'

'Was never much of a beard person myself.'

He told her about the cottage and garden and a little about Elsie and the girl they'd gone on outings with, and her grandmother. He told her about the work he'd been doing. He didn't want to ask about Ginger's brother. She'd tell him in her own good time. As he got up to leave, she said, 'What did you think about Ginger's brother disappearing?'

'Disappearing where?'

'Car parked at that Beachy Head. No sign of a body.'

'Odd.'

'Good bloody riddance, pardon the expression.'

'It was a long time ago, Mum. I don't like thinking about these things.'

He'd never heard his mother swear like that before. She'd often told him she hoped he'd never become like the others with all those horrible words always on their lips.

He phoned his mate. 'What's this I hear about Ginger's brother?' he asked.

'Topped himself. He was a bloody wreck. For the chop, anyway. Here, I'll put you on to Badger.'

'Well, Stanley, young fellow-me-lad,' Badger said. 'Keeping moderately well, I trust?'

'Yes, thanks.'

'So what is keeping you occupied these fine days?'

'I'm moving south.'

'Wise fellow. It's good old España for me. The quiet life, sipping your old G and T by the swimming pool. Well, Stanley, nice to hear your voice, not a day older by the sound of it. But times march on.'

'I'd just phoned to get the gossip...'

'Oh Lordie me, Stanley! Quite slipped the old grey matter. Ginger's brother topping himself. Still looking for the body. Saving you the bother. Very considerate of him. A bad lot he was. Bad as his brother, approximately, anyway.'

'He'd not been well, I heard.'

'Yeah, well, none of us are getting any sprightlier with the passing years, as the saying goes. Must rush, Stan. Keep in touch. And if ever you're bound for España. Hasta la vista, old chap.'

He rang off. It was the first time Stan had known that all along he had hated Badger, nothing but that. Dead scared at first, but then turning him into what he was, making him hate himself, not standing up to him, not standing up to anyone.

Now there was his little room to furnish and his life to begin. He wanted to take something for it from his mother's flat so when he went to say goodbye, he told her that: some little token from a long way back. She thought for a while, shifting and looking around her.

'I know, Stan. Do you see that pig there on the mantelpiece?'

He fetched it. One of the legs was stuck back with brown glue and one of the ears had fallen off. 'It was your first piggy bank. I never threw it away, remembering you rattling it and saving up for I don't know what. You have that, Stan.'

He'd wanted something of hers, not his. Something like a teapot or a vase. He was about to explain that, but then she said, 'I'll just like to think of you putting pennies into it again, the small change adding up. I'll just like to picture you shaking it again. My good little Stanley.'

He took the pig and rattled it. There was a single coin inside.

'It's one of the old pennies,' she said. 'It's the last you put into it. I can see you now...'

She was becoming tired so he went to kiss her on the forehead. 'I'd better start saving again,' he said.

He went to see Sherrill for the last time. The child seemed to have forgotten him and clung to her mother. Stan gave her a thousand pounds, all that was now left of Badger's money. The girl's father had given up coming round, but there was another bloke now, she told him.

'Not more of the same, I hope?' he said.

She shook her head. 'He's good with the little one. I think he really loves me, Stan. You didn't love me, did you?'

'Not enough. Not nearly enough. But enough that I want you to be happy.'

'The money, Stan. I don't know what to say.'

They held each other for a while, the child still clinging to her mother. They did not kiss, but before he left she laid her hand briefly on his beard.

'We're not really beard people, are we, darling?'

The child looked up at him and shook her head.

XVIII

ELSIE PASSED her driving test first time. The examiner told her as if it had come as a huge surprise, after thinking at first she was wasting his time – the way she had to sit right forward to reach the pedals and peered above the steering wheel as if surprised to see a road there. He was ashamed to have thought that. 'The best bit of driving I've seen in many a long year.'

'Now I can visit more gardens,' she said.

'You do that,' he said. 'You do that and good luck to you!'

There were more than a thousand in the book. She had only visited about twenty so far, though one or two more than once, especially Kew Gardens, which was easy to get to on the overland train. Now that she could have a car, perhaps she could visit them all before her life came to an end, ticking them off one by one in the book. It was almost enough just going to

Kew and Regent's Park, her favourite. She got into the habit of taking notes and every time she came back she looked flowers and plants up in the *Gardeners' Encyclopedia*. There were also the wonderful gardening programmes to watch on television. Some of them almost made her cry, the beauty of things and the trouble people took. When she went to see her mother she talked about gardens all the time now. Before, she'd just said where she'd been, as if to give an account of how she'd spent the money her mother had given her, that she hadn't wasted it. Now, she was afraid she might be boring about all the flowers and shrubs she'd seen, but she could tell from her mother's face, usually on the glum side, that hearing about gardens, her enthusiasm for them, was making her quite happy too. 'You must find yourself a nice hobby,' she used to say. And now she had really found one. Sometimes she dreamt of one day having a garden of her own, but it didn't seem quite tactful to tell her mother that. She hardly mentioned her cleaning jobs at all. There was only so much you could say about mops and hospitals and so on. Her mother wouldn't be wanting to hear about all the things that were wrong with the patients.

It was three months before Stan wrote. The card was a picture of an old-fashioned galleon with billowing sails on a stormy sea. He wrote: Dear Elsie. Never was much one for the writing game. Here is my new address. It is thirteen miles from the sea. Quite a nice little flat. I'm doing my gas training and can earn a bit on the side. Regards from Stan. PS. I've still got my beard and still sometimes tell people about my seagoing days!

So now she could send him the picture postcards of gardens. She wrote very little on them because they spoke for themselves. Usually she pointed out some special aspect like the rhododendrons being in flower or a famous rose garden. She always signed off 'Yours Elsie'. He did not often reply, saying that things were ticking along nicely and he was settling in. He always signed off 'Regards, Stan'. He didn't suggest that she might come to visit him.

She nearly did once when she went on a detour to visit Lucy's grandmother. When she opened the door she threw her hands in the air and said 'Elsie! How lovely!' She had never been like that before, always on her guard as if ashamed of something. They sat in that crowded room and drank tea. Twice again Isabel said, 'How lovely it is to see you!'

Elsie sat forward. It was clear what she had mainly come for.

'I expect you'd like news of Lucy?' Elsie nodded. 'They found a lovely little house in Cornwall, near an old schoolfriend with a daughter the same age. A good school by all accounts. They are very happy.' Elsie leant further forward, waiting for more. 'You heard a bit about the marriage, her parents.' Elsie nodded, hating herself for seeming to pry. 'There's the usual sort of messy arrangement, Lucy spending some of the holidays with him, or them, should I say?' She shook her head. 'Poor old Lucy, not being able to say she only wanted to go back to Cornwall, not wanting to bring on one of his tempers.' She closed her eyes and sighed deeply. 'It's better, much, much better than it was. That's the most you can say about life more often than not.'

Elsie wanted to hear more about Lucy. 'She seemed a happy child,' she said. It was one of the most stupid things she could have said.

'Well yes and no... She must have seemed very quiet to you and Captain Stan, she called him, after... after all... awful, awful...'

She did not wish to speak more if it. Elsie looked round and saw the shells neatly arranged on the circular table by the window. It all came back to her, the wonderful days along the seashore, filling the tea towel, the smell of it, the lap and swish of the water, Lucy's big bright smile and her laughter.

Isabel had let the memory pass and looked about her, saying quietly, 'I'm sorry I never spoke to your friend about his life at sea. As you can see, we are a naval family.'

Elsie looked at the portraits and the uniforms with gold and medals on them. She was glad she did not have to reply.

'I've got to go round to see my new neighbours. Why not come along too? See what they've done to the place.'

The woman opened the door and Isabel handed her a pot of jam. 'As promised,' she said. 'Raspberry.'

The woman clapped her hands silently. 'How absolutely lovely!' she said.

'Thank you!'

Elsie moved from behind Isabel, who said, 'I expect you remember Elsie.'

For a moment the woman looked shocked as though Elsie had appeared from nowhere. 'But of course! Of course!'

They went in and stood looking out over the back garden. Everything had changed. The table and chairs were pine now. There were two red-upholstered chairs and a green sofa. There was matting on the floor to hide the woodwork and the curtains were plain gold. The main differences were the bookshelves and expensive looking hi-fi equipment.

'It's looking lovely,' Elsie said.

'We think so,' the woman replied.

But the garden hadn't changed. The brown patches were where they had been before. The shrubs had a healthy look and Elsie wished she had planted more.

And then at the far end of the garden, where the vegetable garden had been, she saw a beautiful summer house. The woman led them out, halfway down the garden, towards it. The door was open and they could see a man sitting behind a desk.

'Amdega,' the woman said. 'The best. All wired

up for electricity and computers and heating in winter.'

It was on a large concrete foundation. The man raised a hand to them.

'Best not disturb,' the woman said. 'He's just getting to the end of his latest. Publishers after him. You know how it is.'

Isabel glanced at Elsie. 'Good solid foundation, I see.'

'Oh yes,' the woman said. 'Base had to be laid pretty deep.' She hesitated. 'Of course! That was your vegetable garden! I remember! Sorry about that.'

'We weren't very good with vegetables,' Elsie said. 'Not in the time we had.'

'Us neither,' the woman said.

They went back into the house. Isabel refused tea, knowing that Elsie wanted her to, or so Elsie guessed from another look she gave her.

On the way back to her cottage, Isabel said, 'Writes the most awful piffle, crime with a lot of romance thrown in. Dreadful. Still, people seem to buy the stuff, so why not?'

Elsie said she couldn't stay for lunch. The image of the summer house stayed in her mind until she returned home.

Stan must have dug very deep. She couldn't stop herself. She kept on thinking how comical it was that a man was writing crime stories there. She thought she must be a horrid person to think like that, of that swish summer house on top of that terrible man. She thought too of the matting covering the wood floor where she'd cleaned up the stain of his blood. That wasn't funny. She looked at herself in the driving mirror and the smile was the same, twisted in disgust; there was no difference.

On her next card she told Stan that she'd been back to their cottage and a summer house had been put up on a concrete base where the vegetable garden had been. She said she thought he ought to know that. In reply he thanked her for her card – of another beautiful big house surrounded by flowers – and said he thought vegetables were overrated in his humble opinion.

She could not send Geoffrey's twins presents for their next birthday because he had accepted a three-year contract in Australia. Geoffrey wanted to tell her that they would miss the very generous presents from their mysterious Fairy Godmother. It could not continue, such a deception, that she was tall and beautiful and did exciting work in the fashion business, or whatever it was they believed. There was an old holiday photograph of her standing beside a donkey and now, one evening shortly before their departure, he showed it to them.

'That's your Aunt Elsie,' Geoffrey said.

They stared at it for a long time. 'Really?' the boy said finally.

'She's a bit ugly, isn't she?' the girl added.

'Yes,' said Geoffrey. 'I'm afraid she is.'

Their mother had left the room, not knowing what direction the conversation might start taking.

'Well, anyway,' the boy said.

'I expect she's really nice,' the girl said.

'Of course she is, stupid,' the boy said.

Geoffrey closed the album. 'Your Aunt Elsie' was all he said.

Dorothy was sad that Geoffrey was leaving. It was only for three years, he said, but they could get to like it and Susan was an outdoor sort of girl. She went to the last of her bridge afternoons the day she heard. After the bridge they had to get hold of bloody Arthur again, mainly for the benefit of a couple of newcomers. They drew the curtains and held hands around the table.

'It's Arthur again,' said Gladys in her moany voice, as if practising it for when she'd be in the afterlife herself. 'He says someone close to home is going on a long journey, a long, long journey... There's someone called Edgar... I'm getting Pooch...'

There was a pause. Dorothy jolly well wasn't going to tell them about Geoffrey going to Australia. Nobody knew anything about Pooch.

'Come along, Dorothy,' Gladys said. 'You must know someone who's going on a journey?'

'Everyone knows someone who's going on a journey,' she replied sharply.

When she left she told them she would be working more time in the Oxfam shop so wouldn't be able to come for the foreseeable future.

'You and your good works!' Gladys said.

Elsie got a job back in the hospital where she'd met Edgar Wakefield. It was there she bumped into him again on his way to outpatients, looking much better. He didn't remember her at first, then struck his forehead.

'Elsie! Just the person! What a coincidence! Meet you in the canteen in an hour.'

He told her he was in a bit of a pickle. His neighbour, Betty Stiles, still thought she would come into his money. She didn't know there was another will. He'd had it drawn up with a proper solicitor and she'd only get four thousand pounds. She was being so kind to him. He wanted her opinion. Should he tell Betty Stiles that the will drawn up at what she thought was his deathbed was null and void? 'It's killing me,' he said. 'Every favour she does me, my laundry, gardening, buying food, the lot.' What was he going to do? Should he come clean? It was getting on his nerves. And to be honest, at his age, he didn't mind the attention. He didn't mind it at all. At last he came to an end. He stared into Elsie's eyes as if the answer was just waiting to be spoken.

'Any good neighbour should do all that, without hope of reward, Mr Wakefield. That is what ordinary goodness is, isn't it?'

'Yes, but…'

'You could write her a little letter to be opened when you're dead, just saying that, and hoping the four thousand pounds would not be taken amiss, her being the sort of person who'd want to be neighbourly for nothing.'

Mr Wakefield slapped his thigh. 'You don't know Betty Stiles, but Elsie, that is where the answer lies. Good advice. Good advice indeed.'

'You'd better be remembering me in your will then, hadn't you, Mr Wakefield? I'll be looking forward to a nice little surprise one day.'

For a moment he took her seriously. He wished he could tell anything from her face. 'I'll bear it in mind,' he said hesitantly.

'Poor old Betty Stiles,' Elsie said.

Mr Wakefield stood up. 'I've got a few years in me yet,' he said.

Later, she chuckled a few times, imagining Mr Wakefield still in a tizzy about whether he ought to leave her a little something in his will.

There was a nice-sounding girl in the office Stan sometimes spoke to on the phone about a gas job. When he met her she was very businesslike. She wore glasses, which gave her a strict expression. She was the sort of girl who came from a respectable family, he could tell. People might say she was plain. She was. But her eyes seemed to look far into things and she smiled trustingly like a child, as Lucy had begun to. It was as if she had suddenly found out how to be happy. There was a thoughtfulness about her too. That was how his mother summed people up: either they were thoughtful or they weren't. They have been out several times. He hasn't tried to kiss her yet but once she put her arm through his as they walked back from the pictures. The next day she kissed him on his beard. 'I like beards,' she said.

And so it is. He will soon have steady work in the gas industry. He is not like other men, she tells him one day, only after the one thing. He does not know whether he can ever tell her he was never at sea in his life, that it was just a joke when someone asked about his beard. He does not know if he can ever tell her he once killed a man. But he knows he must. He would give anything to see Elsie again, to find out what she would think. He does not want to lose this very nice girl. If he told her, everyone might come to know. He should be back in the cottage with Elsie, just the two of them, and Lucy. He had been happy then. What would Elsie tell him? He longs for her...

He went to ask his mother and she said, 'Oh no, Stan, you can't keep it a secret, not from someone you love and who loves you. Once you're sure.' He did not ask her why, because he could tell from her face that she just thought it was completely obvious.

In her next card Elsie said she was going to visit her aunt and uncle in Spain. She wrote: 'It is the most exciting thing in my life so far. It was easy to get a passport, no questions asked about the photo or anything. I've never seen a foreign country before, except on television. They've sent me a ticket and everything.' This time she signed it 'Love, Elsie'.

She did ask her mother if she'd like to come to Spain with her. Dorothy said, 'Not this time, thank you, dear.' But what she thought was: 'Over my dead body.' It wasn't that she didn't want to keep Elsie company seeing the sights and so forth. It wasn't that at all. It was the fancy summer clothing she didn't have and wouldn't know how to choose in the shops. It was also the sort of talkative, half-naked people she'd seen on television with their drinks and suntans and swimming pools and so on. who weren't her sort at all. That wasn't their fault, of course, and they'd probably try to be kind to Elsie, becoming less talkative in the process, distracted from how perfect everything usually was. She'd rather rattle tins outside Tesco's any day of the week, with her own home to come back to in the evenings.

Stan took his girl for a walk by the sea. They sat on a bench and he took her hand and told her the whole story. Her hand stayed there until they saw two children running along the beach with a large black dog. There might be children to tell one day too, and their children. There was her decent, loving family. He knew she was wondering the same thing. And he thought, 'Elsie is lucky, she won't have to tell anyone.'

She took his hand again and held it firmly. He glanced at her and believed that if she had spoken then, she would have said simply that they had all their lives before them to ponder such things.

Elsie sat on the bus, looking out of the window and thinking of Spain. Sometimes now she couldn't help thinking, 'One day I'll turn to the person beside me and say, "I've killed a man." They'd just think I was completely off my rocker and go and sit somewhere else.'